Adventure
Presents

SPICY MYSTERY STORIES

February 1938

Spicy Mystery Stories
February 1938

ISBN: 1-59798-002-1

**This limited pulp reprint edition
© 2005 Adventure House**

**Published by Adventure House
914 Laredo Road
Silver Spring, Md 20901
www.adventurehouse.com
sales@adventurehouse.com**

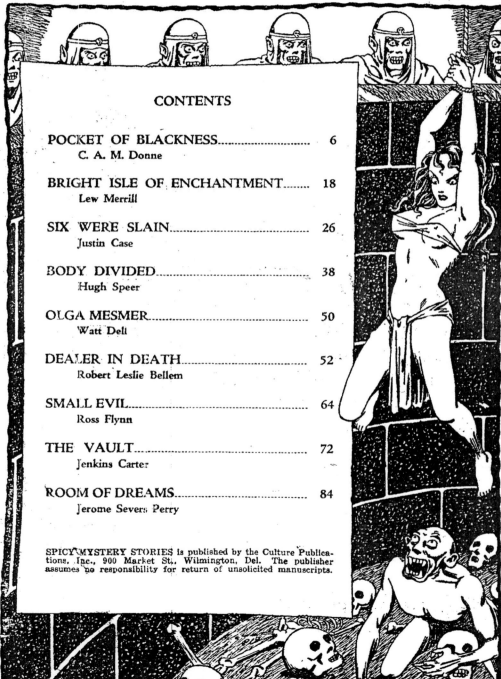

SPICY MYSTERY STORIES

February, 1938   Vol. 6, No. 4

CONTENTS

SPICY MYSTERY STORIES is published by the Culture Publications, Inc., 900 Market St., Wilmington, Del. The publisher
assumes no responsibility for return of unsolicited manuscripts.

LOOK Inside Your Rupture

For the Truth about a Cure

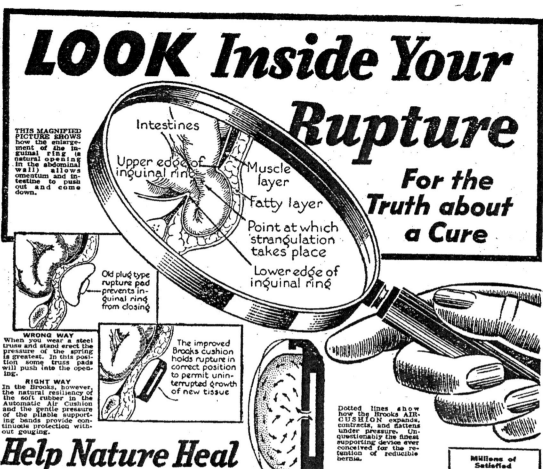

THIS MAGNIFIED PICTURE SHOWS how the enlargement of the inguinal ring (a natural opening in the abdominal wall) allows omentum and intestine to push out and come down.

Intestines

Upper edge of inguinal ring

Muscle layer

Fatty layer

Point at which strangulation takes place

Lower edge of inguinal ring

Old plug type rupture pad prevents inguinal ring from closing

The improved Brooks cushion holds rupture in correct position to permit uninterrupted growth of new tissue

WRONG WAY When you wear a steel truss and stand erect the pressure of the spring is greatest. In this position some truss pads will push into the opening.

RIGHT WAY In the Brooks, however, the natural resiliency of the soft rubber in the Automatic Air Cushion and the gentle pressure of the pliable supporting bands provide continuous protection without gouging.

Dotted lines show how the Brooks AIR-CUSHION expands, contracts, and flattens under pressure. Unquestionably the finest supporting device ever conceived for the retention of reducible hernia.

Help Nature Heal

DO YOU see that bulge of intestinal loops pushing out through the muscular wall of the stomach (abdomen)? That's what inguinal rupture looks like.

The outside wall is skin and fatty tissue. The black wall inside that appears to be broken is the muscular wall. It is not broken. It has a natural opening called the inguinal ring. It is through this ring that your inguinal rupture first appears. Sometimes this ring will close up. If it closes up while your rupture is out you have a "strangulation" and an immediate operation is imperative. If the rupture is being held back at the time the ring closes, then you have what the doctors call a "spontaneous cure." Over 22,000 Brooks users have given voluntary reports of such results.

Now this so called Spontaneous cure is nothing more nor less than the work of Nature. Not in all cases, but in many, Nature will strengthen the muscles and close the opening so that the intestine is held back without further need for any kind of support. But if you will look at the first small picture you will see that such a thing is impossible if the pad

presses into the opening. It is also impossible if the pad doesn't fit just right as it will let a part of the rupture push out.

The Brooks truss invention for the support of Rupture holds in exactly the right position as shown in the second small picture. It is especially designed with this in mind. The soft rubber AIR-CUSHION never presses in—yet it never slips. It gives comfortable and firm support in every position of the body whether you are asleep or awake. Actually it helps Nature Heal for it does not prevent a natural flow of healing blood to the weakened muscles. You can wear a Brooks Appliance on trial and see for yourself whether or not it helps Nature in your case. If it doesn't, you owe nothing. If it does, the Appliance costs you only about as much as you would pay for an ordinary "store truss."

POCKET OF

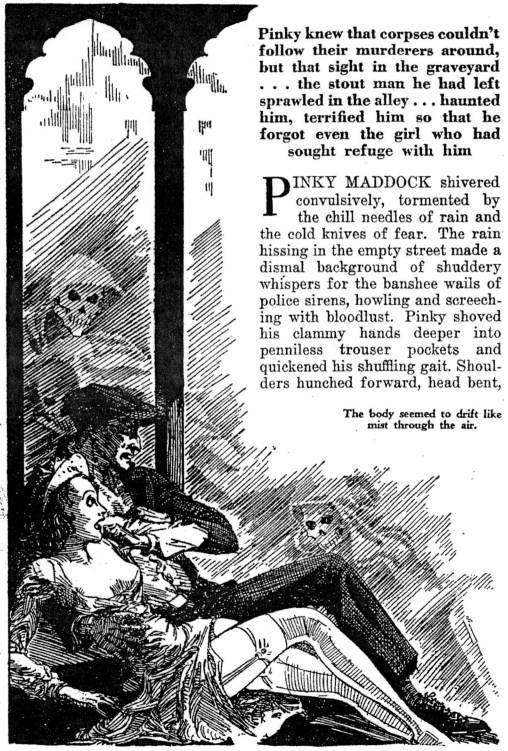

Pinky knew that corpses couldn't follow their murderers around, but that sight in the graveyard . . . the stout man he had left sprawled in the alley . . . haunted him, terrified him so that he forgot even the girl who had sought refuge with him

PINKY MADDOCK shivered convulsively, tormented by the chill needles of rain and the cold knives of fear. The rain hissing in the empty street made a dismal background of shuddery whispers for the banshee wails of police sirens, howling and screeching with bloodlust. Pinky shoved his clammy hands deeper into penniless trouser pockets and quickened his shuffling gait. Shoulders hunched forward, head bent,

The body seemed to drift like mist through the air.

BLACKNESS

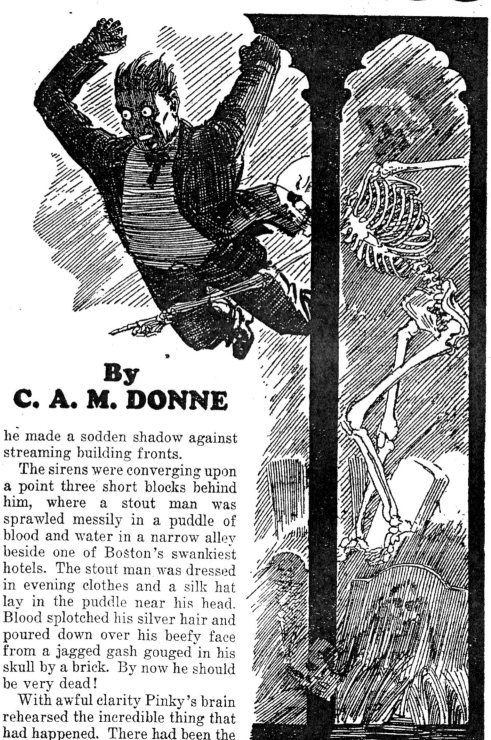

By
C. A. M. DONNE

he made a sodden shadow against streaming building fronts.

The sirens were converging upon a point three short blocks behind him, where a stout man was sprawled messily in a puddle of blood and water in a narrow alley beside one of Boston's swankiest hotels. The stout man was dressed in evening clothes and a silk hat lay in the puddle near his head. Blood splotched his silver hair and poured down over his beefy face from a jagged gash gouged in his skull by a brick. By now he should be very dead!

With awful clarity Pinky's brain rehearsed the incredible thing that had happened. There had been the maddening rain and the maddening gnawing in his belly and a maddening fatigue pressing down upon him. There had been hard-faced cops reminding him that he was only three days out of jail, moving him along when he loitered on benches or beneath awnings, cursing him savagely. There had been the stout man, sleek and warm and well-fed, emerging from the hotel and hurrying along the miraculously deserted street.

"I don't give money to bums," the stout man had rasped, glaring at Pinky's shaking form.

Something that had been stretched too taut in Pinky's brain had snapped. The alley had been right beside them, black as the pit of hell. The strength of insanity had been in Pinky's arm as he grabbed the stout man's coat. They had rolled together on the slippery pavement. Pinky's right hand, which in all his twenty-six years had never done worse than pick a pocket, had closed on a loose brick and his arm had swung it blindly. It had made a queer, dull sound against the man's skull.

Driven by a terrible fear, Pinky had dashed from the alley. A tall young man in a gray suit, standing with a pretty girl just within the hotel entrance, had seen him and emerged to stare suspiciously. That incident had recalled a measure of sanity to Pinky's mind, and once he had turned the corner he had slowed to a walk.

He had opened the wallet he had slipped from the stout man's hip pocket—and hurled it from him, cursing. It was empty. . . .

SOMEBODY coughed beside him. Pinky jumped and crouched, ready to leap away. He turned his scared, skinny face toward the sound and saw a girl huddled in a doorway. She was small and thin and even in the dismal light he could see the drawn lines of her pinched face.

The doorway made a poor shelter. The rain sifted into it, soaking her black dress so that it clung closely to the contours of her body and legs. Frightened as he was, Pinky took time to note the attractions of her figure. It had been a long time since he had known the companionship of a woman. If only he had taken the time to search the stout man's pockets, instead of grabbing an empty wallet and running. . . .

The girl coughed again. She said tentatively: "Lonesome, honey?"

Some of the fear left him. He replied: "Yeah, but I'm broke, babe. I ain't even got a place to sleep!"

She shrugged and said: "That's tough. Neither have I. Got kicked out of my rooming house today, and haven't been able to find a place in this rain."

God, if only he had a room! Pinky passed his tongue over dry lips. Six months he'd been in jail for trying to shoplift some stuff in a big department store, like a damned fool! If he could be alone with a woman like this he could forget those six months, forget that he was in a new mess and the cops were looking for him. He could even forget how hungry he was.

He cursed inwardly and walked on, thinking how soft and white she would be. Warm, too—deliciously warm after the cold rain. . . .

In the middle of the block the mouldy smell of soaked earth and stone filled his twitching nostrils. He was passing a tiny, ancient burying ground tucked into a crevice between tall office buildings— a creepy pocket of silent blackness in the very heart of the city. Through an iron fence gleamed crumbling tomb stones marking the graves of men and women who had lived and died before the Revolution. Back of them rose the bulk of a stone church crumbly with age, its square tower black and grim.

Death— good Lord, there was no escaping it! In the alley beside the hotel; ahead of him if the cops should pick him up and send him to the electric chair—death lurked everywhere, trying to ensnare him. Even here, in the shadows of structures that teemed with careless life during the day, death leered and mocked and beckoned!

THE pallid ray of a distant street lamp touched a tombstone and limned the macabre carving of a skeleton dancing above an illegible epitaph. Such were .the gruesome symbols with which the first generations of Boston men memorialized their dead.

Pinky had a crazy desire to laugh aloud. He wanted to ape the skeleton's ghastly dance—to leap and whirl among the sedate stones, shouting to all the ghosts and troubled spirits, good and evil, to leave their muddy couches and dance with him. What a sight that would be for the cops when they found him!

The cops! There was one, just rounding the corner, his slicker agleam beneath the street lamp. The cop was listening to the hideous music of the sirens, trying to place their center. He was looking around uncertainly, puzzled by echoes. He hadn't seen Pinky yet.

Pinky's hands leaped from their pockets and gripped the spikes of the fence. The gate was secured by a padlocked chain, but it was only waist high. He vaulted it easily and landed with a scrunchy thud on the wet earth beyond. Crouching low, he scurried to the sheltering shadows of the church.

The edifice had a high-roofed porch and the doors were set deeply into the thick walls. In the blackness against the doors Pinky was sheltered from the rain and invisible from the street.

He watched the cop plod past purposefully. There was only one siren wailing now, and presently that sank to a tortured groan and was silenced.

It was almost pleasant lying in the big doorway, listening to the drip-drip-drip of water from the eaves. If only he had something or someone to keep him warm! His teeth chattered as he thought of the girl who had spoken to him. *She* could warm his blood. . . .

A sound at the iron fence struck new terror to his heart. He sat up and stared wide-eyed at the dark figure squeezing through a narrow opening where the end of the fence did not quite meet the wall of a building. As the figure moved toward him with swift stealth Pinky's scalp prickled. What manner of creature would be prowling an ancient cemetery at midnight?

A cop, or a ghoul—or something not even human?

But it was the girl he had been thinking of. She came onto the stone porch, her dress plastered wetly against her legs and hips faithfully outlining every curve. She wasn't as thin as he'd thought. Pinky could hear her hard breathing.

He whispered: "Hello, babe."

She clutched her hands to her bosom and gasped. For an instant he thought she was going to scream. Then she recognized him.

She said: "The cop told me he'd run me in if I didn't beat it. I saw I could get in here and thought maybe there'd be a dry place."

"Sit down," he told her. "It's dry here."

She sat so close beside him he could feel the faint warmth of her body through her clothes. He caught a whiff of cheap perfume.

"It's cold," she said.

He cleared his throat awkwardly. "I won't be cold much longer, sitting this close to you ... !"

The girl laughed. "Nothing slow about you, is there, buddy?"

"No. I been lonesome too long, and I never was no angel!"

"Me neither," she said, sighing. "I used to try to be, but life's been too tough. I don't get the breaks, I guess."

He put an arm around her clumsily. He pulled her close and she put her head on his shoulder. His eyes, accustomed to the darkness, could see vaguely the vee of her dress, cut low above the shadowed whiteness of her breasts. His heartbeat quickened and his breath came faster.

"Lonesome," he repeated. He put his other arm around her and held her closely. She yielded with seeming reluctance at first, then lifted her lips to be kissed. Pinky tasted cheap lipstick, but to him it was like nectar. All the stifled emotions of six months welled up within him.

He muttered: "Jeeze, I'm glad you came in here!" He pulled at her until she rested half across his lap, her shoulders cuddled in the crook of his arm. She bent one knee and her damp skirt slid upward. Pinky could see the faintly gleaming whiteness of a shapely thigh.

He wasn't cold any more. He wasn't hungry. He wasn't afraid. . . .

WEIRD brilliance flooded the little cluster of graves minutes later, ushering in fantastic horror.

Pinky had made a damp pillow of his coat and lay on the worn stone threshold of the door. He wasn't cold because Sara—her name was Sara Lane, she had said—was close beside him. There was still the smell of dankness in the air and the drip-drip-drip of the rain from the eaves, but Pinky's fears had vanished and for the moment he was content. Morning would bring another day. Maybe there would be some way of earning or stealing money and getting a room. Maybe Sara would be content to stick with him. That was what he needed—somebody sweet and feminine, like her. . . .

Then the brilliance forced itself upon their closed eyes, blinding them even through the lids. Pinky could see it almost as brightly as though his eyes had been open. At

Holding the light high, he placed the knife against the girl's shrinking flesh.

first he thought it was lightning, then he knew it couldn't be. It lasted too long—a full half-minute, he guessed. It was an eerie, blue-white glare that seemed to pierce e v e r y t h i n g it touched—that seemed to touch his limbs and body like a thing of substance.

Then enveloping blackness again in this pocket of blackness in the heart of the city—save for the wheels of blue fire that seemed to spin before his dazzled eyes, confusing and bewildering them.

A choked cry, not loud but freighted with spine-chilling horror, rang briefly through the cemetery and echoed from the walls of the surrounding buildings. There was a thud, a gurgle and a *crack* like the breaking of a stick not far away.

The short hairs at the base of Pinky's neck bristled. His throat was dry and his eyeballs ached with the effort of trying to see through the flares that filmed them. For a reason he did not even try to fathom he was more frightened than he had ever been in his fear-spotted life—far more frightened than he would have been if he had seen a platoon of cops advancing on him through the tombstones.

Frozen there, he kept one arm tight around Sara. He could feel her soft breasts rising and falling with tremulous breathing. From her throat came an almost inaudible whimper, telling him her terror was as great as his own.

For a full minute—perhaps two minutes—they sat there, not moving, not daring to utter a word, clinging to each other.

By that time Pinky's vision cleared a little. He could see the buildings rising toward the overcast skies at his right and left, their windows closed and expressionless through the transparent curtain of rain. He could pick out the individual grave markers, chipped and toppling and rotting. Nothing seemed changed anywhere.

Yes—there *was* a change. Over there at one side of the graveyard, just behind the table-like monument that marked the resting-place of a Revolutionary hero, something bulky lay on the dank grass. It was only a blob of shadow, formless and motionless, yet it seemed charged with a nameless dread.

And while it repelled him, it drew him as the hypnotic eyes of a serpent can draw a bird to death. Wanting to run, and keep running until he had left this hell-steeped cleft of perpetual midnight far behind, he knew at the same time he could never rest until he had seen what the thing was.

HE FORCED a tight whisper through his constricted throat. "Wait here fore me—babe."

She pleaded piteously: "Don't go! Don't leave me!" She was watching the blob of shadow, too, her eyes dark pools of dread.

But Pinky had already left her. He dared not delay, for he knew his nerve would desert him the instant he relaxed. And he *had* to know what the fearful thing was!

Mud clutched at the soles of his worn shoes with a sucking sound. The rain began to fall harder, driving into his face as though to force him back. His hunger and weariness returned. The soul-shriveling fear of being caught and convicted as a murderer came back to him.

And still he forced his lagging feet toward the monument that barely concealed the object. A gleam of light reflected from a window-pane struck the top of the stone vaguely, bringing out the skull and crossed bones engraved in its surface. The sign of death!

God, the world seemed full of death tonight! The very air Pinky breathed was dead. He felt like a man who had ceased to live.

Just around the stone, now, on the other side, lay the shape. He could take just one quick look and dash away. A man was afraid of the things he didn't know—not of the things he faced squarely and understood. This was probably just something he had overlooked in his first view of the burying ground. It was probably—

His blood congealed in his veins. His heart gave one mighty leap and stood still, frozen in horror. His skin seemed to shrink, crushing the flesh and bones within it. He wanted to scream, but his throat was dammed by incredulous fear. He wanted to flee, but the power of motion had left him.

Before him in the grass, just as he had seen him last, lay the stout man he had left sprawled in the alley behind the hotel. His evening clothes were spattered with blood and mud and his silk hat, dented at one side, lay near him. His silver hair and his face were streaked with blood that had come from a deep gash in his scalp. And his ghastly eyes, wide open in death, looked straight into Pinky's convulsed face!

It couldn't be! Corpses couldn't follow their murderers around, haunting them. Ghosts didn't exist, except in mad people's imaginations—and if there *were* ghosts, the ghost of the slain man wouldn't appear to Pinky in this guise. It would be a gray, stealthy thing, like—

Like that moving object at his right, near the church!

In a way Pinky was glad he had glimpsed the eerie prowler through the foggy darkness. It was fearful enough, considering the time and the place, but it helped him take his eyes from the hideous corpse and enabled him to draw a long, shuddering breath into his starved lungs. The gray thing wasn't coming toward him; it was slinking along beside the stone edifice, seeming to drift like mist through the air just above the ground.

A moan of sheer terror forced its way through Pinky's lips. He took a step backward, away from the accusing eyes of the dead man. He took another step, more rapidly. Another, grateful that at least he could move—and then his heel caught in something and he fell with a smothered scream.

His desperate fingers clawed into the grass. One hand closed on something moist and clammy. Pinky didn't want it, whatever it was, but his fingers would not unclench. Stark insanity was beating at his brain. He scrambled upright, his fists pulling up chunks of sod. He ran across the slippery earth, permeated with death—not toward the fence and escape, but toward the church. He needed the warm touch of Sara, the feel of live, human companionship.

SHE was sitting as he had left her. He dropped on his knees and pillowed his head on her breast. His breath came in great sobs. He was like a scared child running to his mother.

Sara put her soothing arms around him. He felt her slim body move close against him. She was warm, comforting. He'd get her out of this accursed place. They'd find a room or a corner of the city where they could be alone, where there would be no dead things pestering them, bringing madness.

He babbled: "We gotta go, babe! Stay with me! God, I'm afraid!"

Her voice showed her fear, too, but it was steadier than his. She said: "You're sick, guy! You need a bed and something to eat. I'll get you to the city hospital. When you're better I'll look you up, if you still want me to."

"No!" He couldn't bare to think of that. He needed her now, continually, forever. Supposing she *was* no angel—a woman, down on her luck and desperate, willing to take a chance with the first person would could give her any kind of a break? He was no angel, either. Why, he had killed a man, and he couldn't get away from it!

He clung to her frantically.

"What's that you got in your hand?" she asked.

He forced his fingers open. Grass and dirt fell from his right hand. His left held wet, wadded paper, and as he stared at it his eyes bulged. It was money. A dozen or more bills of large denomination. Tens, twenties, fifties!

He muttered: "You take it! I mustn't keep it! The dead guy— he brought it to me because I missed it before. It's my pay for killing him! The wages of sin. If I take it, it's death for me!"

She took the money, counted it swiftly and put it inside the bosom of her dress. He had a glimpse of the white mounds of her breast as she tucked the roll between them. Then her hand went to his forehead.

"Four hundred and eighty dollars," she whispered. "It's a hell of a lot. I'll take care of it for you till you get better! You got a fever now. I'll get a room for us and call a doctor. I won't run out on you!"

He struggled up. "Let's get going! We can't stay here!"

"Wait," she warned, putting her fingers over his working lips. "We can't go right now. Somebody's coming."

He stared with sick eyes across the expanse of old graves. He saw two shadows coming toward them. Both were gray, misty, stealthy. It was too much. He couldn't keep on fighting hell's hosts forever.

"Ghosts," he said. "It's no use, babe. You beat it! I'm licked." He was thinking: *She'll find somebody else. . . .*

He leaned wearily against the heavy door of the old church— leaned and felt the solid oak swing inward behind him. He gasped and a new wave of fear engulfed him as hands grasped his shoulders.

"God!" he shrieked. "God!"

Something struck him heavily across the top of his skull. A blaze of red light seemed to fill his brain. All his body went numb. He heard Sara scream thinly. As consciousness left him he was certain the strange hands out of the blackness were pulling him straight into hell.

HELL! There was a weird, flickering light all around him, like the luminescence of a decomposing

Pinky's hand closed over the knife, as claw-like fingers sought his throat.

corpse. Pinky's tongue was dry and swollen, his head ached abominably, his stomach heaved with nausea. When his eyes could focus he saw beside him a dripping wall of ancient stone. His nostrils filled with the odor of decay.

He felt curiously light-headed and wanted to laugh. So hell was at the bottom of one of the ancient crypts—or was it in the cellar of the old church? At any rate, it was in hallowed ground, and there was a dreadful humor in it. The same kind of humor there was in the dancing skeleton on the tombstone he had seen—the ugly figure sorrowing relatives of another day had thought appropriate for the last couch of some beloved kinsman.

And Satan tied men's hands and feet in hell! Pinky found that out when he tried to move, because his shoulders were against the dripping wall and a rough edge of stone pressed into his back painfully. His wrists and ankles were bound with heavy cord.

He was not alone. There were four others in the stone room with him. Sara lay in slimy mud beside him, bound as he was and mercifully unconscious. Rough hands had torn her dress at the shoulder, so that one round breast was partly uncovered. Her skirt was tumbled above her knees and her thighs gleamed above the tops of cheap silk hose.

Another girl, bound similarly, was stretched across the top of an unpainted table. She was young and pretty, with fair hair and blue eyes that were wide with fright. Her dress was in shredded tatters. A tiny brassiere cupped small, firm breasts and flimsy step-ins clung to her white, shapely hips, only half concealing them. Her skin, at her throat and waist and thighs, was milk-white.

The tall young man in the gray suit—the same who had been talking with a girl in the lobby of the hotel and had stepped outside to watch Pinky flee from the alley—was lashed with rope to a chair. His gray eyes blazed in his lean face and the hinges of his jaws bulged. He kept watching the girl on the table.

Pinky's flesh crawled when he looked at the fourth person. He was tall and cadaverous. Through slits in a black domino mask, black eyes flickered balefully. His clothes were soiled and shabby. He held a tallow candle aloft in one hand and a glistening knife in the other.

As Pinky watched, the masked man put the point of the knife against the throat of the man in the chair. He chuckled ghoulishly.

He said: "Why shouldn't I slit you open? I got my getaway all planned. But I might be good to you—if your girl decides to be a good sport . . ."

The girl on the table cried suddenly: "Don't touch him! I'll do anything you say. Only promise you won't hurt him!"

"Damn you!" grated the man in the chair, glaring at the leering face above him. "If you touch that girl, I'll break these ropes and strangle you with my bare hands. If you kill me first, I'll come back from the grave and drive you crazy!"

The other chuckled again. "You're nuts about her, aren't you? That suits me fine. You spoil my racket, so I spoil your sweetheart. That's fair enough, isn't it?''

"Please!" moaned the fairhaired girl. "Get it over with. Do anything you want with me, but don't torment Gordon any longer. You can make your getaway, and someone will find us here tomorrow and free us.''

The black eyes behind the mask turned toward her, roved the whole length of her lovely body. The saturnine mouth in the gaunt face twisted and the tip of a tongue appeared, moistening the thin lips. The man stuck the candle in the neck of a bottle on the table.

"Okay," he said hoarsely. "Watch me, Thane."

"Oh, Tess!" the man sobbed, his eyes and face tortured. "Let him kill me instead! I don't want to live at that price!"

"No price is too much for your life, dear," the girl said. She closed her eyes and shivered as the cadaverous man's fingers touched her white shoulder.

CONFLICTING emotions surged through Pinky. His first thought, when he saw the point of the knife press against the throat of the young man in the gray suit, was: *Now he'll never be able to identify me, and he was the only one who saw me run from the alley.* Then a wave of revulsion engulfed him; he didn't want to see the young fellow die—he looked like a good sort. Even though he himself was a murderer now, Pinky wasn't reconciled to killing.

Then, when Pinky understood what the evil-faced man intended to do to the girl on the table—the

girl the young fellow called Tess— a new kind of aversion filled him. Jeeze, that was worse than murder, if anything could be!

And maybe the fiend would turn his attention to Sara, too. After all, Sara wasn't to be overlooked. Her clothes might be cheap and her face might be pinched by worry and hunger, but in spite of all that she was enticingly pretty. Her hard mouth would soften after a few weeks of right living—the kind of living Pinky would see that she got, if ever he got out of this mess.

For Sara was his girl. He'd made up his mind to that! Pinky wouldn't have said it in so many words, but he was in love with her. If they didn't snag him for bumping the stout man, he'd get a job and go straight and make her a good husband.

But first he'd have to figure some way out of this smelly hole in the death-filled earth—some way out of this circle of hellish events that had converged upon him. He'd have to get free and free Sara and lead her up into the rain again, out past the sprawled corpse of the stout man, past cold-eyed policemen and to some sort of shelter. Maybe, after all, no harm would come of his using the money he had picked up among the rotting sepulchres.

The sharp point of masonry made a throbbing pain at the small of Pinky's back. He moved a little and his bound wrists came in contact with it. Sudden hope welled up within him.

The gaunt man fixed him with a gimlet eye. "You! Sit still," he ordered, "or I'll slash you wide open!"

(Continued on page 103)

Bright Isle of

From the wreckage of their plane in mid-Pacific, that man and that woman were privileged to visit realms and see things unknown to all living mortals

CAMPION and Lady Molly were flying low now because their gas was almost exhausted, and they were scanning the boundless wastes of water under them to find the little isle that was their destination.

Campion was at the controls in the front cockpit. Thirty-two, American, two trans-Atlantic flights to his record, and an expert navigator. Lady Molly Deventer sat back of him, an earl's daughter, and a free-lance almost since she had been born. Newspaper woman, aviatrix, and no young girl now—thirty years old.

The thing that had brought the two together was that love of danger that is a part of the love of life. The flight across the Pacific, from

All the women he had ever loved were there to welcome him.

Enchantment

one tiny island to another, was something nobody had ever attempted. Nobody had tried to fly the Pacific from south to north, from New Zealand to Honolulu.

And they were not lovers. Just good sports who had met at a New York night club, where both were being feted by an admiring crowd, and, on the spur of the moment,

decided to make the trans-Pacific flight together.

Charley Campion looked at Lady Molly in her bare-backed evening frock, swept his eyes over the superb curve of her breast,

By
LEW MERRILL

studied the lovely lines of her body, the black-sheathed limbs beneath the lilac skirt, and he knew. He understood. He recognized the spiritual quality in the woman that made her more than a mere feminine creature, and knew she didn't care a damn who saw and admired her, because the physical in her was subordinated to the spirit. Love, adventure, danger, death— yes, but you would have to win that dauntless spirit to yourself before she would surrender in complete abandonment.

Would she ever do so? Well, these were modern days, and Lady Molly was a woman of thirty. One doesn't speculate about women's virtue in these days. It's altogether too crude. And Charley Campion didn't care a damn.

BECAUSE, at thirty-two, he took life as he found it, and being a healthy male, he took his pleasure in the way of the twentieth century, with mirth and fun and happiness, and no romantic nonsense. All that was closest to Campion's heart lay buried in the seething waters of the Atlantic.

He had been madly in love with Nora Clinton, who had made that crazed flight from Ireland with Hubert Crane, two years before. They hadn't even had a radio set. And the plane had never been heard of since. Nora and Hubert had perished in the watery wastes somewhere between Ireland and Newfoundland.

And Lady Molly had been engaged to marry Hubert Crane. That was what had brought the two together at the night club in New York.

Lady Molly said, "So you're the man who was engaged to Nora Clinton. She told me about you. She said it was to be her last flight. I've wanted to meet you for two years past. You knew I was engaged to Hubert?"

"Yes, I heard that," said Campion.

Lady Molly leaned toward him. The loose neckline of her frock momentarily revealed the first gentle fullness of her bosom just below the whiteness of her throat, and, because she had brought back Nora Clinton so vividly to him, he was stirred only by the sense of comradeship with a woman.

"I've only one regret," said Lady Molly. "Death is natural and inevitable. But I loved Hubert as I shall never love anybody again. And I never really knew him as I would have liked to. That's bitter, Campion. It's the negation of life."

"If I had, and could remember that, I could take whatever life holds for me. I don't know if there's another life, or if I'll ever see Hubert again. But I can never belong to him completely now he is dead. Do you see how it hurts me?"

"Why didn't you?" Campion ventured to ask.

"Because I loved him so much, I was afraid. Afraid to break the beauty of our relationship. It was everything in the world. And—he died."

Then they talked about Campion's projected flight from New Zealand to Honolulu, and Lady Molly offered to accompany him and split the expenses.

They traveled together on the

boat from San Francisco, and they were the best friends in the world. It was natural enough that they should kiss sometimes. Of course, everybody thought that they were lovers. But they weren't. Each had the memory of a dead love. Campion had tasted other loves, when they came his way, without in the least diminishing his heartache for Nora, but he was convinced that Lady Molly had lived for the memory of Hubert Crane —would always do so.

LADY MOLLY leaned forward, peering at the instrument board in the light of the setting sun. "We'll have to go down, Charley," she said. "The gas will be gone in five minutes."

Campion shouted back, "I'll ease her down, Molly. We'll float till we're picked up. Nothing to worry about."

The plane was fitted with pontoons, and was made to float for days, unless a storm came up. There were canned foods, and a small barrel of drinking-water. But the chances of rescue in that remote part of the Pacific were improbable. Both of them knew the situation.

And neither cared. They loved life, but each of them had his dead. For Campion, Nora Clinton, dead two years in the Atlantic waters. For Lady Molly, Hubert Crane. You can't get away from your dead. You may be a hard-boiled old business man, but the mother you worshiped when you were a kid is still living in some way, still exercising some influence over you from beyond the grave. You may be a down-and-out, and there

is the girl you used to take buggy-riding fifty years ago, who married another man and died, an obese grandmother. It doesn't matter. You can't get away from your dead!

Campion cut the gas and eased the plane down. "There's a storm," he shouted back at Lady Molly. "We'll make it." He blew her a kiss, because their comradeship was very gallant and gay. But each knew that this was the end. There was no land in sight, and the waves were surging under them, and the wind whistling through the struts and trying to upset the frail craft of the air.

Each of them was thinking of his dead. Campion of Nora Clinton, and Lady Molly of Hubert Crane. They were both built that way. The kind of people who don't believe that death is the end.

You don't have to have any particular religion to believe that.

There wasn't a chance. It wasn't possible to gauge the wind direction for alighting. The airplane dropped like a plummet into a thousand tons of seething water.

SOFT air, soft grass beneath him —and Campion stared into the face of the old man beside him.

It was a beautiful face. It was old, but it had power. It seemed the face of one who had chosen to be an old man rather than a young one. And it was a face that was vaguely familiar to Campion, although he could not place it. It seemed to him that he had known the old man very intimately all his life.

He started up. "Molly!"

"She is safe and well," said the old man.

"Where is she?"

"Being taken care of."

"And where am I? How did I get here? God. I thought we were sunk!"

"You floated ashore. This island hasn't been charted yet. It is inhabited by people who are untouched by civilization. Once, aeons ago, it was part of a vast Pacific continent."

"You're a damned good fellow to have pulled us ashore," said Campion. "But I must see Molly at once and—I suppose the old crate cracked up?"

The old man nodded, but there was a singular look in his eyes, as if a child were speaking to him. Suddenly Campion cried, "Do you mean that we are dead?"

"There is no death," said the old man.

"We're dead! We're dead!" cried Campion.

"There is no death," said the old man again.

"Where in God's name am I?"

"I'll show you."

THEY walked across a meadow gorgeous with spangled flowers. At the far end, beneath the palm trees, young men and women were walking to and fro. There was nothing to suggest lovemaking in their attitudes. Diaphanous draperies seemed to clothe them. To and fro across those meadows. . . .

"God, Nora!"

The old man's hand tightened upon Campion's arm. "Keep still!"

"Nora! We must be dead! She died!"

"Yes, she died," said the old man.

"Am I dead?"

"Not yet."

"I want her. Oh God, I want her!"

"But she is dead," said the old man.

"I can't go to her?"

"Did you read, when you were a boy, of the myth of Orpheus and Eurydice? He went down to hell to bring back his beloved wife. And he was told that he could take her with him *if he didn't look back.*"

"Well—yes, I remember something about it."

"He looked back. No man has ever brought a soul out of the Plutonian realm without looking back —and losing her."

"I want her!"

"Look at her," said the old man. And Campion looked at Nora Clinton, his dead love, strolling on those meadows of asphodel, with other souls.

"Oh my God, I want her!"

"If you don't look back!"

"What do you mean?"

CAMPION'S guide took him by the arm. "I mean, my dear fellow, that life and death are nothing more than day and night. One finds one's own again—always. But, if you want her back in an earthly life, it can be done only by a miracle. It is only through the gates of birth that dead souls come back to earth."

"She is dead, then?"

Campion's guide bowed his head.

"Why can't I get her?"

"Why couldn't Orpheus get his wife, Eurydice, in the Grecian myth? Because, my dear fellow, God has set the gates of birth between incarnations. Because *you would look back!*

"I'd never look back," said Campion.

The old man smiled. "There she is," he said. "If you can woo her and win her, she is yours."

And then Campion saw Hubert Crane, strolling among the shades, and Lady Molly clinging to his arm. Campion hadn't perhaps guessed how deep Lady Molly's devotion had been to the dead aviator. He saw her holding his arm.

As the lashing of the surf lessened, they made to shore.

But he forgot her in his love for Nora Clinton.

His guide released his hold upon his arm, and he crossed the fields of asphodels. As he moved, the figures about Nora moved away, leaving her alone.

Campion stood staring at her. And she stared back at him in a dim, wondering way, as if she faintly recognized him.

"Nora, it's Charley! Oh, Nora, darling, I've been wanting you for so long!"

"It's—Charley," Nora whispered.

"Don't you remember me, Nora? Don't you love me any more?"

"Yes, but you—you're not dead yet, Charley. Not dead like me!"

THERE was infinite pathos in the look she gave him. "Charley, of course I remember you," she said. "But that was in the old life and the old life's gone."

"No, I'm going to take you back," said Campion. "Do you remember once I told you I'd win you out of the jaws of death itself? I'm going to do that now."

She smiled for the first time, and placed her hand upon his arm. He turned toward the old man who had guided him, moving slowly across the meadows. But suddenly he was only dimly aware of Nora. For he knew that shape gliding toward him, coming between them.

The form of a woman, nude, save for a foam-like wisp about her hips, firm breasts that he knew so well, and supple waist—little Daisy Carroll, the show-girl of Broadway, with whom he had consoled himself after Nora's death. She came toward him, a smile upon her face, her arms extended for an embrace.

"You — dead — ?" whispered Campion.

"Not yet," she answered. "Just asleep and dreaming of you, Char-ley. Hoping you won't forget me when you return to New York."

For an instant Nora was forgotten in the remembrance of those weeks of rapture with Daisy. She had been new to the ways of life and—well, he had recompensed her well, and the flame that she had kindled in him burned up again, hot and strong. Then he was again conscious of Nora at his side, and the memory of that undying love of theirs made him forget Daisy.

She seemed to vanish then, and, with Nora's hand still on his arm, Campion pursued his way toward the old man, who was still waiting where he had left him.

But they were following him like shades. That red-haired beauty, with the white bosom and enticing limbs, was Polly Noonan, with whom he had spent a whole week in her penthouse on Fifth Avenue during her husband's absence.

Jack Noonan had never amounted to much, wasn't worth bothering about, and certainly not worth scruples of conscience. But Campion hadn't known Jack Noonan was on one of his trips with some transient love, when he called at the penthouse apartment to discuss the matter of the new propeller his firm was making for his plane.

Polly had opened the door to him, wearing a dressing-robe, evidently fresh from her bath. And the two, looking silently at each other, had suddenly known what didn't need any words. They two, man and woman, had looked upon each other, and liked what they saw.

"Mr. Noonan?" Campion stammered.

"He won't be in today."

"I'm Charles Campion."

"Yes, I know. I've seen your picture in the papers."

Then she had laughed and gone into Campion's arms. The loose robe that had covered her before, fluttered free, unheeded, to half bare her lovely body with its sculptured bosom and sleek white thighs.

He had picked her up and carried her into her room, and then followed a week of madness, sheer ecstatic madness, before Campion went away.

"Where are you?" Campion whispered.

"In the penthouse, asleep. Dreaming of you," she answered.

And then again Campion became aware of Nora at his side, and of the touch of her hand upon his arm, and, because she meant more to him than all the women whom he had known during his bereavement, he turned resolutely away. And now he could see Lady Molly and Hubert Crane moving toward him, through a crowd of flitting forms.

"Don't look back!" he called. "Don't look back, Molly!"

AND now a new slim white figure stood before him, so close that their bodies almost touched and he felt her warm breath on his cheek. A girl's laughing face was thrust forward toward his own. Red lips, white teeth, little breasts that had flattened themselves against him in ecstatic moments. Kay Wynne, the showgirl who had been his constant companion for a brief spell, after Nora's death, and had married the Florida millionaire after they had broken off.

Nobody had stirred him as Kay had done, though it had been a thing of the flesh, and not of the soul as in the case of Nora. Their friendship—Campion was recalling every detail of it—had begun at a night club when the rest of the party, seeing their attraction to each other, had left them to themselves.

(Continued on page 113)

Six Were

When Avencio brought the beautiful statue to the under-ground fortress, none of the five guards knew that death and madness were the penalty of touching the Virgin of the Sun

GRACIAS, *señorita!* With all my heart I thank you. It is a long time since I last smoked a cigarette. A long, long time. No, no, no, do not light it for me! If I light it now, it will be gone too soon. Let me just hold it in my lips for a while. When you are gone, then I will be lonely and I will need it. These four walls close in on me, sometimes, and make me cry out for mercy.

26

By JUSTIN CASE

Slain

"They told you, I suppose, not to listen to me, eh? I am mad, they say. I have murdered six men and I am dangerous. Perhaps. But I will not harm you, my good friend. Sit here, here beside me if my cot is not too filthy for you. Let me look at you. You have a kind face, and there is wisdom in your eyes. You are very lovely.

"I am a soldier, *señorita*. You know that, I suppose. What you are I know not, except that I was told you would come to visit me before I am led before the firing squad. I was told you come often to talk with the prisoners. That is kind of you, *señorita*. Very kind. You are so beautiful. Permit me to stare at you, because it is the last time, perhaps, I shall ever be permitted to watch the red quivering of a woman's lips or see the soft

27

swell of a woman's breast. I had a sweetheart once, *señorita*. She used to nestle in my arms, with her lips hungering for mine. Her dark hair would caress my face. Her warm body would tremble against mine, and we would whisper love-words to each other. But that is finished now, and I but bore you with it. You came to hear my story, no?

"But first, *señorita,* move closer to me. It is lonely here! Ah, that is better! Your head upon my shoulder, so. My arm around you. Do not be afraid! I am not mad; I am merely human."

WE were soldiers in the army of Greco Zamidas, *señorita*— I and Avencio and Jose and the other two. Of the war itself I can tell you nothing, for I did not fight in it. For two whole years I hardly knew there *was* a war, except when supplies were brought to us at that remote jungle fortress and we were able to question those who brought them.

I cannot tell you of what happened in Quasa del Jara, where the army of Greco Zamidas fell before the rebel horde. I cannot tell you of the assault upon Maridas, where the rebels were butchered and the streets ran red with blood. You know more than I about those things. Me, I was buried all that time.

It was a strange place, *señorita,* and to this day I know not why we were kept there to guard it. Greco Zamidas himself did not build it. It is older than your great-great-great grandmother, and was perhaps built by the Aztecs.

Here is the jungle. See, I draw a map for you in the dust at our feet. Ah, your feet are tiny, *señorita!* So tiny and lovely, like the rest of you! Now then, the river winds through the jungle, so. For hundreds of miles in all directions there is only swamp and forest. And here, here beside the river, in the heart of all that desolation, is the fortress.

Not above ground, *señorita*. Ah, no! Above the ground there was once an Aztec city whose remains are still festering there. The fortress lies beneath, and we were sent there to guard it, lest the rebels seize it. Do not ask me why the rebels might desire it, *señorita*. I am only a soldier. I do not have the intelligence of the men whose orders I obeyed. Enough that we were sent there, the five of us, and that for two years we lived there like outcasts, knowing nothing of what went on in the world of the living.

Jose, Avencio, Mario, The Young One, and Pancho—we five—we lived there. We slept together in one vast underground chamber. We played cards, drank ourselves drunk when the bearers of supplies were kind enough to leave us liquor. We were men, and there were no women. We were lonely. I, Pancho, who tomorrow must face a firing squad, was in charge.

Is it for pity you come closer to me, *señorita?* If so, I humbly accept, though there was a time when women trembled against me with passion, not pity! I kiss your hand. I ask your lips. Ah! . . . *Señorita,* I *will* be insane if I do not return to my story! The sweetness of you is a drug! The nearness of you, the warmth of your trembling body.... Remember, I have languished in this foul prison for weeks, with no outlet for my emotions!

But I was telling you, *señorita* . . . there were five of us, and we lived in that weird underground world of darkness and silence. At first we took it as a joke; it was our palace and we were the masters of it. .There was little work to do, and we were paid well. We thought of our brothers fighting and dying in the war, and we pitied them.

Then we began to be lonely. Jose, he had a wife; he missed her. At night he would dream of her and mutter in his dreams. "Ah, my darling!" he would say. "It is so pleasant to have you beside me, so! You are so warm, so soft. Come closer, and press your lips to mine. Put your arms about me!" And he would wake up with beads of sweat glistening on his face, his fingers clutching at empty space. He would stride back and forth, cursing all of us for laughing at him.

Avencio, he joked and made mock of the rest of us. Never in his life, he said, had he loved any woman. What he had never had, he would never miss. "I am a man's man," he used to say. "I need only mescal and tequila to keep me contented." He drank like a pig.

The Young One, he had a sweetheart and longed for her. Have *you* ever been lonely, *señorita?* Have you ever moistened your lips for a man's kiss, when there was no man to kiss you? Have you not ever yearned for a man's gentle caress? Then you must know how The Young One felt, and how I felt, for I, too, had a sweetheart.

WE grew to hate the sight of one another. We cursed one another, and as the days crept by like snails, we tried to avoid one another. And then the fatal night was upon us—the night when Avencio went above ground and brought back the marble statue.

It was a beautiful thing, *señorita.* Beautiful—like you. Where he found it I do not know. He would not tell us. He was drunk when he went exploring, and I suppose he was drunk when he came upon the statue. Quite likely he discovered it in some secret chamber of the old Aztec temple.

He brought it back to us. Staggering under the weight of it, he came shouting and singing down the long, torchlit corridor of our underground fortress, and stumbled into our sleeping room, and set the statue on the floor. "Now," he jeered, "here is a woman! You need no longer complain of the loneliness!" And when I say to you, *señorita,* that for a moment the silence in that room was deafening, you must believe me.

It was a life-size statue of a woman, this one, and I could have sworn it was alive, so amazing was the genius of its maker. She stood there with her arms outstretched to us, her lips parted in a faintly scornful smile. A creature so gloriously beautiful *had* to be alive! It could be no mere lump of cold stone!

She was young, *señorita.* As young as you. Her breasts were tantalizingly arrogant, as if she had just drawn a deep breath and were daring any of us to touch her. The yellow glow of our crude lamps slanted down upon her, and in that weird half-light she was wonderfully real. I could have sworn that her eyes were watching us, that her lips moved. Those deliciously feminine shoulders were never made of stone! Those mature young hips, sweeping so divinely into long, tapered legs, were surely trembling!

We gathered around her, while Avencio sprawled down on a bed and leered at us. He pitied us, accused us of being little children with vast appetites. He made mock of us. When I turned on him and ordered him to be quiet, he jeered at me.

Remember, *señorita*, I was his commanding officer. I could have shot him down like a dog. Perhaps I should have. But he was drunk, and I overlooked his insults. After all, he had brought us a companion.

That night I heard a voice whispering in the darkness, and said to myself: "Jose is dreaming of his wife again." I lay awake, listening. And it was not Jose. It was The Young One, talking to the statue. I leaned out of my bed and saw him, and pitied him.

He was on his knees, *señorita*, at the feet of our beautiful lady. His head was tipped back and he was staring at her tantalizing form, and his great mop of hair was like a shimmering black column of smoke, because every inch of him was trembling with desire.

He caressed her as if she were alive. He hugged her close to him and his clumsy fingers wandered over her marble curves, tightened about her slender waist. "I've been so lonely," he whispered to her. "Night after night I have dreamed of you until I thought I would go mad. Now you have come to me, my beloved. Now we love each other again as we did before."

He kissed the tips of her fingers and stood up and took her in his arms. For a long, long time his mouth was on hers, and I could hear the hoarse wheeze of his breathing. You see, *señorita*, he *was* mad. He thought the marble angel was his sweetheart.

I sighed and went back to sleep, pitying him. In the morning, perhaps, he would be sane again. But in the morning, when I tried to arouse him from his bed, he merely turned over upon his stomach and ignored me. Had I not known him so well, I would have dragged him to his feet and cursed him for being drunk—or drugged.

He did not awaken until late that afternoon, and even then he merely sat there staring at the statue, without a word for any of us. Jose, finding me alone in one of the corridors, said bluntly: "What ails The Young One, Pancho? Is he sick?" And I did not know the answer.

That night The Young One again made love to his "sweetheart". And the following day, while we were swilling down our dinner, I realized how mad he was.

IT WAS a miserable dinner, cooked by Mario who was not so adept as the rest of us in preparing vile food in a manner to camouflage its vileness. Avencio was very drunk. He sniffed at his plate and pushed it away from him, making faces at it. He seized a bottle of tequila and said loudly: "A man would have to be staggering drunk to eat such slop as this! Therefore, my pigeons, I shall drink until I am too drunk to eat at all!''

We laughed at him, all but The Young One, and our laughter swelled to a roar when he leaned from his chair and drunkenly put an arm around the statue's waist. "The lady and I," he said, "will get thoroughly drunk together! Yes, my angel? No?''

I glanced at The Young One and saw that his fists were clenched and his face was white. I should have

The woman knelt there, raised her arms to the moon for a moment.

ordered Avencio to be quiet, I suppose, but my God, how was I to know what would happen?

Avencio lurched up from the table and held the woman close against him. His gaze roved drunkenly over her breasts, down the gentle swell of her stomach. He pressed his wet lips against her marble cheek.

"We will get drunk together," he grinned. "Very, very drunk, my angel. Here! This is for you!"

So saying, he tipped the bottle of tequila to her mouth, and caressed her beautiful body with his free hand while the liquor trickled down over her chin and throat to the shadowed valley between her breasts. Had she been alive, we might have turned away in disgust; but since she was merely a creature of marble, we thought it a huge joke.

All but The Young One. He, with a strangled roar of rage, leaped to his feet and hurled himself at Avencio's throat, overturning the table as he went.

It would have been murder, *señorita*. Avencio, even though drunk, would have seized The Young One in his big hands and crushed every bone in the boy's frail body. Therefore I rushed between them, thinking to keep them apart. But I underestimated the boy's madness.

He flung me aside, and I tripped over an outthrust leg of the table. He swung his fist to Avencio's face, and releasing the statue Avencio staggered back, blood trickling from a corner of his mouth. It was ghastly then, *señorita*. The Young One rushed at Avencio and Avencio seized him, shook him so savagely

that we could hear the brains beating against his skull. The boy clawed blindly at Avencio's face, and kicked him, but Avencio held him off with one hand and with his other hand drew a knife.

I knew what would happen then. A quick thrust of the blade, a cruel twist, and The Young One would sink to the floor, screaming with agony and holding both hands over the wound to keep his intestines from gushing out over the room. So I drew my gun and roared at Avencio to desist.

He did not hear me, or if he did, he was too drunk to pay attention. The knife gleamed. I took aim and squeezed the trigger.

And that, *señorita*, is how I murdered the first of the six men whose deaths are charged against me. Ah, yes, I do not blame you for shuddering. I do not wonder that your soft breast trembles against me, or that your warm, yielding body quivers in my arms. But you see— it had to be done.

AFTER that, *señorita*, I ordered Mario and Jose to take the statue out of our sleeping room. I ordered them to carry it to the end of the number three corridor, which leads to the ammunition chamber, and leave it there. And as punishment for his part in what had happened, I ordered The Young One to bury Avencio and we built a huge stone cross over the grave.

Three days passed. All was peaceful. The Young One maintained a strange silence, speaking only when spoken to. Mario and Jose and I played cards, and I made out a report to send back when next a messenger came with supplies.

Then one night a monstrous desire crept over me, *señorita.* A burning hunger to feast my eyes again upon the alluring loveliness of the marble woman. I frowned at myself for entertaining such thoughts, but when the other three were asleep I slipped out, took a torch, and went to her.

She was there where Mario had placed her, and when I gazed at her I knew that I was not the only one who had been to visit her. That perfect body was marked with the prints of greasy hands. Those smooth, flawless curves were finger-smeared.

It saddened me, *señorita,* and it angered me. I resented the thought that any of my comrades had dared to caress my woman. Yes, she was *my* woman. I loved her.

I crept back to the sleeping room and obtained water, and with my handkerchief I washed her lovely body. Ah, how gentle I was! As gentle as though she were alive and could feel the touch of my hands. As gentle as I would be if *you, señorita,* were to come to me with bruises upon your gorgeous body that had to be attended to.

And I knew who had made those marks upon her. Only yesterday I had ordered Mario to clean and oil the machine-guns which guarded the entrance to our underground world!

After that I watched Mario every moment. I said nothing, but I watched him. The following night, when he thought we were all asleep, he slipped out of his bed—and I followed.

He went to the marble woman. He knelt before her, kissed her lovely feet, then rose and took her in his arms. I heard him whispering to her. And then, as God is my witness, *señorita,* and may my soul crawl on its belly in hell if I am lying, I heard another voice, *and it was hers!*

The marble woman had come to life!

Jealousy gnawed at my soul as I watched them, yet I had not the courage to step forward. I thought I was dreaming. But Mario took that lovely, yielding form in his arms and glued his lips to hers and held her as I might hold you, *señorita,* if you were less afraid of me.

I saw her pale flesh quivering to his touch. I saw her once-rigid breasts cushion upon his chest as would soft flesh. Her white arms crept around his neck and she pushed him gently against the wall of the corridor, held him there with the pressure of her arching body while her seeking mouth drew the very soul from him.

I said to myself, scornfully: "She is like all other women. She is no goddess, but a creature of base desires and passions." Yet I envied Mario his exquisite torture. I loved that woman myself!

Then she took Mario by the hand and led him along the corridor. They passed within arm's reach of me, almost, without knowing I was there. And I followed.

SHE led him above ground and into the crumbling ruins of the old Aztec city, and like a skulking dog I moved after them. There was a moon, *señorita;* an enormous golden bowl in the sky. And there were strange, weird mutterings in the jungle, and faint bird-cries from the dense weeds along the riverbank. I had a feeling that I was walking in a world that was not of tonight but of a night many, many years ago. I am no coward, yet fear festered within me.

She led him, I say, into the ruins of the city, and I wondered where they were going, for I myself had explored those ruins many times and knew of no spot romantic enough to lure a man and his woman. If they sought romance, why were they not walking the other way, where the river might lull them into pleasant dreams with its whispering voices? But no, they stopped in what might have once been a narrow courtyard.

The woman knelt there and raised her face to the moon for a moment, and I drew a sharp breath of appreciation. How beautiful she was, with that soft golden glow laving her glorious form! How I longed to take her in *my* arms and press my eager lips against hers!

She placed her hands upon a broken stone column then, and the column moved. I saw an aperture widening before her. Saw a flight of stairs leading down into blackness. She descended, and Mario followed. The aperture closed behind them.

Then, *señorita, I* tried to follow, but my eyes had deceived me and though I struggled with that broken stone column for more than an hour, cursing it and beating my fists against it, I could not solve its secret. Like a madman I stormed about the ancient courtyard, shaking my fists at the moon and reviling Mario for having stolen my woman.

In the end, exhausted and drenched with sweat, I returned to our buried fortress and flung myself down on my bed. The Young One and Jose were still asleep.

It was my weariness that saved me, *señorita*. I was too tired to close my eyes, and too full of hatred to desire sleep. When I heard those whispering footsteps in the corridor, I knew at once that something was wrong.

It was not Mario who was coming, or if it was, he was making a great effort to reach the sleeping chamber without being heard. The footsteps were far apart and full of guile. And when I saw that it *was* Mario, and saw the knife gleaming in his hand, I snaked a hand to my belt and drew my gun.

There was madness in Mario's eyes, and it was not the kind of madness that comes from loving a woman too much. His lips were curled back and his white teeth glistened in the dim glow of the lamp that was still burning against the far wall. On the threshold he hesitated, glanced first at me, then at the others. On his toes he crept toward The Young One.

I held my breath, while a dew of cold sweat formed upon my face. The Young One's bed was directly across from mine. He slept like a baby, with a smile on his face that told me he was dreaming of the sweetheart for whom his heart hungered.

Mario bent over him. The knife glittered like a thing alive. I tried to cry out but had no voice. I had only a gun with which to prevent the awful thing that was about to happen.

I squeezed the trigger. What else could I do, *señorita?*

That is how Mario died. So you see, *señorita,* two of the six murders of which I am accused were really not murders. Avencio and Mario died at my hands, but not because I wished to destroy them. There was nothing else I could do.

Later, *señorita,* The Young One and Jose and I examined that knife. It was a sacrificial knife with strange designs carved in its golden hilt. I spent many hours won-dering where Mario had found it.

WE buried Mario and we missed him. He had been a good soldier and a good companion, and his inexhaustible store of jokes,

"Take it," she whispered, "and destroy your companions while they sleep."

though ribald at times, had kept us amused in our loneliness. That night I went to the end of the corridor that led to the ammunition chamber, but the marble woman was not there. I made up my mind to forget her.

It would be as easy, *señorita*, to forget *you!*

I went above ground, seeking her. Hour after hour I spent in that weedgrown courtyard, until I thought the eeriness of the place and the maddening voices of the encroaching jungle would twist my mind. And then one night about a week after Mario's death, the woman was waiting for me when I crept from our underground world to go looking for her.

We stared at each other, and neither uttered a word. I took her in my arms. I had known her and loved her from the beginning of time, it seemed. The thrill of her yielding body was not a new sensation but a repetition of some half-forgotten delight which I had first experienced centuries ago.

Her long, soft hair caressed my corded arms as I crushed her to me. Her breasts were warm and vibrant, and her body melted against mine as though it were soft wax flowing into a mold. When she kissed me there were live coals in my heart, searing me with a wonderful agony.

How long we were there in the darkness I do not know, for time had no meaning and life stood still. I sometimes wonder how much of it was real and how much a dream, but what followed, *señorita*, was no dream! Ah, no!

As she had led Mario into the courtyard, so she led me, and this time I stood beside her while she embraced the broken stone pillar. I saw how it was done. A touch of the fingertips, so. A quick twist of the hand . . . so . . . and the earth opened at our feet.

The stone stairway seemed endless, and the darkness that enveloped me was like a great black fog against my eyes. Yet when I hesitated, my marble woman whispered words of persuasion, promising me things for which any man would have sold his soul to Satan. And so I followed her.

We journeyed a long way through the Stygian gloom before the inky darkness was relieved by light. Frankly, *señorita*, I was afraid and would have turned back, but apparently my lovely guide could read my thoughts, and each time my fears became exaggerated she slowed the pace so that my groping hands might find her and discover anew the glory of her. And so we came at last to a vast underground chamber, where light filtered down through slanting slits in the roof far above us.

We were in the subterranean vaults of an ancient Aztec temple. That part of the temple which lay above ground had long ago succumbed to the elements, but the part in which we stood was ageless. All about us were glittering images of gold. The floor under our feet shone like a sea of sunlight. When I uttered a cry of amazement, my voice returned to me from everywhere and was a long time dying.

Here was wealth for the taking! And here beside me was a woman with soft, clinging arms and throbbing breasts, a woman whose matchless beauty had already enslaved my soul to her wishes.

I forgot that Mario had been here before me and emerged a madman. When my glorious companion led me, with a promise in her liquid eyes, to a shadowed niche I went eagerly. When she drew me to her and I felt the eager, yielding pressure of her milk-white body burning against me, I cast aside all fears and surrendered utterly to the mad joys of the moment.

A man can forget anything for love, señorita. If you, for instance, were to hold out your arms to me the way she did, I might forget that tomorrow I must face a firing squad! No? Not yet? Then I will finish my story.

We were there a long while, señorita. A long, long time. Her lips drank from my soul and her melting body drove me to a frenzy. When she left me, I closed my eyes and slept, and she awakened me upon her return by fusing her mouth with mine again.

In her hand she held a knife. A knife, señorita, like the one with which Mario had tried to murder The Young One. "Take it," she whispered, "and destroy your companions while they sleep. Then there will be none left to disturb us or to threaten our love."

I looked at the knife and felt a slow shudder creep through me, but when I stood up, señorita, the blade was gripped in my fist. If my glorious sweetheart wished me to kill Jose and The Young One, so be it! Her slightest desire was my command.

"I will wait here for you," she whispered. "And when you return, my very soul will be yours, to do with as you will!"

I wondered if I would be able to find my way out of there without a guide, señorita, but I need not have wondered. My feet knew the way and made no blunders. It was as if I had walked through that fearsome darkness many times before, if not in this life then in some remote existence of which I had no recollection.

I CLIMBED the mysterious flight of stone steps, señorita, and made my way across the ancient courtyard. The night had worn thin and the first faint shafts of gray dawn transformed the sacrificial knife in my hand into a coldly murderous thing that seemed hungry for blood.

I crept along the corridor of our underground fortress and curled my lips with satisfaction when I entered the sleeping room. Jose and The Young One had not even missed me. They were sound asleep.

I would have killed them, señorita The soldiers who flung me into this vile prison say I did kill them, but I say to you I would have killed them. A merciful god was watching over me, to prevent it. He caused me to stumble on the threshold, and in stumbling I lurched against The Young One's bed.

The Young One came awake and saw me, and flunk back the blankets that covered him. "What are you doing?" he said sharply. "Pancho! What is the matter?" And his voice awakened Jose.

They seized me and I did not resist, for the sharpness of The Young One's tones had shattered a great bubble in my brain, and I

(Continued on page 106)

·⋮⋮⋮⋮· BODY

There was something queer about the girl that stumbled
into his cabin that night . . . but Don Lancaster could
not know what made her an angel one minute and a devil
the next

DON LANCASTER, seated in his cabin in the gloaming, pouring over the sheets of his half-finished novel, heard what sounded like some animal pattering down the trail through the scrub, and looked up.

He started to his feet with a cry of astonishment. It was a girl, no more than twenty years old, barefooted, wearing a nightdress that had been ripped by the thorny undergrowth. One of the rents half exposed her breast, across which the jagged tatters hung, and through the skirt of the nightdress

DIVIDED

By HUGH SPEER

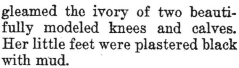

gleamed the ivory of two beautifully modeled knees and calves. Her little feet were plastered black with mud.

With a cry, the girl stumbled forward, caught at the door-jamb, toppled. Don sprang to his feet just in time to catch her. As he supported her in his arms, he could

Don sent the knife upward with all his strength. At the same instant Purvis' panic-shaken hand squeezed the trigger.

feel the trembling warmth of her limp body, and the soft contours pressed against him made his heart beat a little faster.

She looked up at him with a piteous, woebegone expression. "I'm Mary!" she cried. "I'm Mary! Mary Emerson of King Hill. Don't let them tell you I'm not! Don't listen to them! I'm Mary Emerson —Mary!"

Don lifted her little figure bodily in his arms and put her down gently upon the camp cot in the single room of the shack. The sheer beauty of her, the raven hair that cascaded about her shoulders, the litheness of white limbs beneath the nightdress thrilled him with the sort of thrill that any man would have felt under the circumstances; a thrill however that in Don was combined with pity. For he knew who she was.

He had learned that from the village storekeeper during the two weeks that he had occupied the old shack by the lake. The insane Emerson girl, who was looked after by her uncle, a nurse, a physician, and a male attendant, in the big house on King Hill. The daughter of old Emerson, the tobacco magnate, who had left millions in trust for her.

He had seen Emerson, the uncle, a surly, scowling brute on horseback. Deliberately Emerson had let the horse splash mud over him.

There had almost been a brawl when Don remonstrated. Emerson had threatened Don with a riding-crop. Then he had thought better of it.

"You'd best get out of that shack. We don't want loafers around here!" he shouted, as he turned his horse's head away. That had been four days previously.

DON drew a blanket over the girl now, and looked at her in perplexity, as she lay staring up at him.

"I'm Mary," she kept saying. "Mary Emerson. I'm Mary!"

"Nobody is going to harm you here," said Don gently. "What's the matter? Why did you run away?"

"I ran away from her. From Betty. She was going to whip me again. See, see what she's done to me!"

The girl was evidently distraught, heedless of where she was, or that she was talking to a man. She flung the blanket aside and slipped the tattered nightdress from her shoulders, revealing herself to the waist. Don saw with horror that, while one side of her body was unmarred, the other side, and exactly half her back were criss-crossed with the livid scars of a lash-thong.

Had the insane girl been subjected to that treatment in the house on King Hill? A furious anger began to burn in Don's heart. Who could have exposed her to that shame and torture, except her attendants?

As she sat there, staring at him as if bewildered, Don noticed a singular thing. One of her eyes was bluer than the other. One was blue-gray, the other was gray-blue. In the darkness the difference was not striking, certainly not disfiguring or disharmonious. And Don remembered having seen a man with one brown eye and one blue eye. Such cases were uncommon, but not infrequent.

But he also saw that one side of her bosom was a little fuller than the other. There was a very slight, but unmistakable, disproportion, and Don remembered Lombroso's theory that criminals and those not mentally normal invariably showed a certain physical asymmetry.

He pulled the tattered nightdress up about her shoulders and covered her up. He made her lie down. He would have to inform her uncle somehow, but of course he couldn't leave her there alone. She was plainly dazed, obviously a case of schizophrenia, in which the patient lives in a withdrawn world of his own.

"Lie still and rest," Don told her.

"I'm Mary," she kept repeating. "I'm Mary Emerson. I'm afraid of Betty. Keep Betty away from me!"

ONE thing to do struck Don Lancaster. It was perhaps a ridiculous thought, but Don couldn't bear to see those little feet and ankles splashed with mud. He got a basin and filled it with water. He carried it to the side of the cot, a towel over his arm, and proceeded to remove the dirt.

Beautiful white arched feet appeared under the coating. Don handled them tenderly, and again love and pity struggled within him.

It was nearly dark now. He could no longer distinguish the slight difference in coloring of the girl's eyes. The cold water seemed to soothe her, and she lay still. Don could see that her eyes were open, and that she was staring up at the roof. He could catch that faint muttering now and again, "I'm Mary! I'm Mary!"

What, he wondered, was the hallucination at the back of that persistent statement?

He had finished his job, and was wiping the little feet, when he became conscious of a shadow darkening the entrance. A tough, ugly-looking man was standing there; a man in a striped suit, looking rather like a pug. He strode into the room and uttered a derisive laugh.

"Enjoying yourself, ain't you?" he sneered.

Don stood up. "Maybe," he said. "But I don't know you've got the right to ask me." He'd never seen the fellow before.

"You'll learn. I'm Pugh, Miss Emerson's nurse, detailed to handle her when she's in one of her violent spells. If there's any footwashing to be done, me or Miss Masson will attend to it. Get that?"

He strode to the side of the cot and jerked off the blanket.

"Come along, young lady," he said. "We're going home."

The girl sat up with a scream, her hands seeming to go instinctively to the scarred side of her body. Why only one side? That thought flashed through Don's mind for an instant, and was immediately replaced by another. Was it Pugh who had lashed her?

Don clenched his fists. Pugh swung about, his own fists doubled.

"Listen, fool," he said, "I'm used to trouble. That's what I'm hired for."

TWO more men were coming into the darkening room. One of them Don recognized as Emerson, the man whose horse had splashed him. The other was a small, furtive man with a black beard. A medico, at first glance.

"Here she is!" shouted Pugh. "Caught this slob washing her feet for her. Gawd knows what he'd have been doing next, if I hadn't come along. He seems to be getting up steam for trouble."

"Damn you!" shouted Emerson. "I told you we don't want loafers around here. You're letting yourself in for a mess of trouble, you fool, interfering with my ward."

"Maybe," answered Don. It was on the tip of his tongue to speak about the lashings, but he managed to refrain. Instinct told him that that card had best be played later. "What are you accusing me of?" he asked.

"Wait a moment, gentlemen. Wait! This is just a misunderstanding," interrupted the doctor, coming softly forward. "You see, Mr. Lancaster," he addressed Don, "this poor young lady is demented. No doubt she fled down the trail to your cabin without realizing what she was doing. I think, Mr. Emerson," he continued, "Mr. Lancaster was probably taken aback and did what he considered best under the circumstances."

It was oil on troubled waters. But there was something unctuous about the medico's manner that Don didn't like. And then, those marks of a whip on Mary Emerson's side!

"I am Doctor Purvis, in charge of Miss Emerson," continued the little man. "Let me thank you for giving shelter to this unfortunate girl. Come, Betty!" he addressed her sharply.

The effect was electrical. The girl leaped to her feet, a smile upon her lips.

"Yes, doctor?"

"We're going home, my dear."

She glanced at Don, suddenly aware of him, coyly pulling the nightdress about her shoulders. "You haven't introduced this gentleman to me," she pouted.

"Another time, my dear. Mary's at home, waiting for you."

"Mary!" A cruel smile curved her lips. "Oh, yes, I must certainly get back to my darling sister. Another time, then!"

She turned to Pugh, who raised her in his arms and left the cabin, carrying her back along the trail. Don, stupefied, revolted, watched her clinging to the pug, saw his hands tighten about her slender waist and under her bare knees, and because there wasn't anything that he could do, he just watched till they disappeared into the darkness.

MARY! Betty! which was she? Why had she sought protection from Betty under the name of Mary, and then answered to Betty's name? Were they two sisters, or were there two personalities in the girl?

The big house on King Hill stood as gaunt and bleak by day as by night. Don had learned that the tradesmen were not admitted beyond the big iron gate. A homicidal maniac was supposed to dwell within, guarded by the doctor and the man Pugh, and the nurse, Miss Masson while Emerson appeared and disappeared at intervals.

Don couldn't think of the girl as a homicidal maniac. He remembered the piteous way in which she had turned to him in his cabin. He remembered the little feet that had fitted so snugly into his hand. And the lashes! If it hadn't been

Don rushed at Mary, tore the whip from her hands.

for those whip-marks, Don might have been content to let the matter go.

But he couldn't let it go! He didn't like the personality of any of the three men who were guarding the girl. He spent days prowling about the scrub in the lowlands around the hill, looking up at the big house, always silent, apparently deserted, and he could learn nothing.

The novel remained untouched. Day and night, Don brooded over the situation. Somehow he felt that the girl and he were destined to meet again. But he never imagined that the meeting would occur in a short time, or take on such a surprising form.

H E HAD stretched out in his clothes after returning from a prowl around the house on King Hill, and fallen asleep before he knew it. He started up, at a low trill of laughter, to see her standing in the entrance to his cabin, bathed in moonlight.

She was dressed this time, in a neat frock, with silken stockings and heavy shoes, and her laughter was very different from the piteous pleas she had made that former evening.

He moved toward her and stopped, staring at her. Her eyes looked exactly matched in the moonlight. Two small breasts were apparent beneath the frock, but, if one side of her body was formed any different from the other, Don couldn't see it now.

"I'm Mary. Don't you remember me?" she whispered. "I've come to thank you, and to ask your help. Won't you help me?"

She rested her hands lightly upon his shoulders and looked into his face. She laughed again. Don's heart beat rapidly at her closeness to him—and yet somehow it seemed to him that she was more like the "Betty" entity than the girl who had pleaded to be saved from her.

"They call me mad. I am not mad! They keep me drugged, because they want to get my money when I come of age; Cyrus Emerson, and the people he's employing. If you'll help me escape them, take me to Waynesville, my lawyer there will protect me. I swear I'm not mad, except when they keep me drugged. Will you save me?"

Her arms went around his neck, and suddenly Don felt her soft body crushed against him. His breath came faster. Yes, this was Mary, the girl he loved.

"I'll do anything I can to help you," Don promised.

"Tomorrow night, half an hour before the moon rises. If you go around to the back of the house, you'll see a pathway running down to the cellar door. *That door's unlocked!* I managed to get the key, unlock it, and put the key back. Nobody guessed that I had come out of the drug that devil, Doctor Purvis, gives me. I found out that he administers it to me in my glass of wine at night. I spill it into a flower pot and pretend to fall asleep. They don't watch me closely enough to detect that. I'll be waiting for you. Will you help me? *Will you?*"

Her lips were moist, sweet, on Don's, and shudders ran through her warm, slender form as she clung to him.

"They'll think I'm asleep. We can steal away to the village. Roberts, the garage-man, is my friend, and he knows I'll pay him well. He'll have a car waiting for us. I got a message to him. You'll help me?"

"Of course I'll help you," answered Don. "But who is Betty? Who dares to whip you?"

"Miss Masson, the nurse. She's a fiend! She tortures me for the pure delight of torturing. They let her do as she pleases. Oh, I can trust you then?"

"I swear it," answered Don.

"Then I must go." She tore herself from his arms. "I must get back in case anyone becomes suspicious. I— Oh, I love you!"

She was gone, leaving the warmth of her body and clinging lips, and the alluring fragrance of her, to haunt Don through the rest of the night, and all the following day.

THERE was about an hour of darkness before the rising of the moon. Don threaded the trail through the marshes at the bottom of the hill, until he was opposite the rear of the house. Then he moved softly upward until he stood at the rear of the great, gaunt building.

There were lights in some of the rooms in front, but the rear was entirely dark. The windows stared blankly, like dead eyes, out of the rear façade. It was so dark that it was several moments before Don could discern the ramp running down between two brick walls, apparently leading to the door Mary had described.

He moved softly along it, and found the door. He tried the handle, and found that it was unlocked, as the girl had promised. He called softly, "Mary!"

There was no answer, but suddenly he heard a moaning, sobbing sound coming from somewhere within the house. Now Don could see a thread of light beneath a door at the far end of the passage.

He crept softly toward it. Then the unmistakable swish of a whip sounded, and again that moaning. A chill of horror shot through Don. Was that arch-fiend, the nurse, whipping Mary? Forgetful of all prudence, Don ran swiftly to the door and hurled himself against it.

It burst open. He found himself in a sort of laboratory. A dynamo was purring softly; there was some electrical apparatus on a long table, a couch and a chair. But Don hardly saw these things. For in a recess Mary stood, nude to the waist, one hand fastened to a ring that hung from overhead. In her other hand was a whip. *And she was whipping herself!* At every swish a moan of agony broke from her lips; then they would curve in a derisive smile, and the free hand would raise the whip again. Thin red lines were appearing beneath one breast, and drops of blood were trickling down one side of her back.

Watching her was a woman of about thirty-five, in a nurse's uniform; a dark, thin, saturnine woman, with a mocking smile on her face.

As Don burst in, she swung around and screamed. Don ignored her, rushed at Mary and snatched the whip from her hand. The girl sagged, suspended by one arm from the ring; she had fainted.

Then something hard and heavy dropped on Don's head, and a brilliant rocket burst in his brain and swept him into darkness.

HE knew he had not been out more than a few minutes, but he had been entirely out. It was the drag upon his shoulder muscles that revived him. For a few moments it seemed to him that he hung suspended in space. Then, as the reeling room began to steady, he perceived that he was hanging with both hands tied by a rope to the iron ring, his feet brushing the floor as he swung slowly to and fro like a pendulum.

Emerson and the man Pugh were standing across the room, watching him. Doctor Purvis was seated in a chair, writing at his desk. The nurse, Miss Masson, still with that mocking smile upon her face, was bending over the girl, who lay unconscious on the floor. She had fallen sidewise, and on the bare arch of her back and beneath one of her breasts were the red weals from the whip.

As Don opened his eyes, Emerson stepped up to him leering.

"Waking up, eh, loafer?" he sneered. "Well, take it easy. You're going to die in about five minutes. You stepped right into the trap Miss Emerson laid for you, and you've nobody but yourself to thank for it."

Don gritted his teeth. It was the knowledge of Mary's having betrayed him, rather than the threat of death, that made his thoughts bitter.

Purvis got up and came toward him, stood plucking at his black beard. "You're Lancaster," he murmured. "The man who wrote that series of amusing stories for a magazine last summer about a girl with a dual personality. Based, no doubt, on what you had read of the famous Sally Beauchamp case. Interesting, but technically incorrect. You scribblers should never dabble in medicine.

"I've always thought I'd like to meet the author of those stories and show him a real case of dual personality. It's a pity you've got to die, Lancaster, but you *would* prowl around the house, snooping into our affairs. Still, I can't let you go before I've explained this very interesting medical case to you."

"Aw, cut it out, doc!" snarled Pugh.

"No hurry," said Emerson suavely. "She's still out. Go ahead and amuse yourself, doc. You'll never get over the lecture-hall habit, will you?"

"YOU see, my dear Lancaster," purred the doctor, standing before him and wagging his forefinger, "every human being is really two persons, for the median line separated him into two halves. All that they share in common is some of the internal organs, which are of very ancient genetic origin, and are controlled by the sympathetic nervous system. But apart from these, we have two separate sides to every human body. And, what is more important, two separate brains, absolutely distinct, with a median cleft between them.

"You may have noticed that one of this poor girl's eyes is of a

The knife touched his shirt.
"Kill him, Betty," Purvis said.
"What are you waiting for?"

other words, the two personalities that should have united to form Miss Emerson have played independent roles throughout her life. And for a very simple reason.

"In normal human beings, what unites these two entities is the *corpus callosum,* a band of fibrous texture that joins the two sides slightly different tint from the other. There are also certain slight asymmetries, when measured by the Bertillon method. In of the brain together. In a few rare cases, this fibre does not exist. We then have two distinct entities in one body, as in the case of this poor, unfortunate girl. And we are apt to have slight asymmetries in the development of the physical organism.

"Mary is a sweet girl, but pretty much of a dumbbell. Betty, a little devil, hates Mary like nothing human. If they could have been united by the existence of this band of fibre, Lancaster, you would have a normal woman. As it is, you have two sides of a human body, hating each other.

"By electrically stimulating either side of the brain, I can produce either the Mary or the Betty entity at will, for a short period. Betty was in the saddle when you burst in, and taking it out on Mary. I'm going to keep her in the saddle for a while—and that's just too bad for you, Lancaster. Because she's going to kill you, poor demented girl. Betty's got no sense of a moral code at all!"

Don didn't answer. Hanging there helplessly, he realized that his chances were absolutely nil. He was watching the girl, who was now coming back to consciousness. She tried to sit up, and Miss Masson supported her, her arm around the girl's shoulders.

"I'm Mary, Mary," moaned the girl.

Miss Masson slapped her hard across the cheek, and shook her. Purvis moved forward, carrying a coil of wire attached to a battery beside the dynamo. He adjusted a clamp to one side of her head.

"No, no," moaned the girl.

"Take her away. I'm Mary, Mary, Mary!"

Even then a little thrill of joy shot through Don. He knew now it was the "Betty" entity who had lured him into the trap, but he still believed in the "Mary" entity, and loved her.

HAVING clamped the attachment to the girl's head, Purvis went back to the dynamo and threw a switch. The purring became a humming, a shower of green sparks flew from some instrument upon the table. And slowly the girl's expression changed! The cruel smile that Don had seen that night in his cabin was beginning to curve her lips.

"Did I hurt the little fool? Did I whip her well?" she asked Miss Masson.

"I'll say you did," answered the nurse, kissing her. "Look, look, darling!" She pointed to the red weals on the girl's side.

Don realized that the electrical stimulus had again put the "Betty" personality in command.

"Where's that damned little dumbbell?" the girl demanded.

"Oh, she's gone away," laughed Miss Masson. "But her boy friend's here."

"Her *what?*"

"Her boy friend. How would you like to kill him?"

"Oh God, I'd do anything in the world to get even with the little fool!" shrieked the girl.

Don saw Miss Masson pull a knife from the bosom of her frock and thrust it into her hand. The girl sprang to her feet and moved crouching toward where he hung. Her breasts, her entire curving, sinuous body seemed plumper, fuller than when she had been "Mary". Bare legs and feet beneath the short skirt revealed every motion of her hips. A sneering smile curled her red lips. Eyes were fixed on Don's in abysmal hatred.

Then she stopped short in front of Don, holding the long butcher-knife, and looked back toward Purvis.

"Kill him," said the doctor softly. "Don't be afraid of him. Run in and thrust it through his vitals. Twist it! Don't be afraid, Betty!"

The girl turned toward Don again. They were all watching her, the nurse, the doctor, Emerson, and the man Pugh. It was like a scene in a play, fantastic even to Don as he hung there.

He could raise his feet and kick her, but that would be all. The single movement would leave him hanging, twisting grotesquely in the air, at the girl's mercy.

"Kill him, my dear," said Purvis. "What are you waiting for, Betty?"

She swung about again, drew back the knife, her lips parted in the same cruel smile. Her eyes met Don's.

THEN suddenly, miraculously, the look on her face seemed to change. Suddenly she rushed forward with a cry. But, instead of plunging the knife into his body, she slashed madly at the ropes that tied his hands to the rings; slashed three, four times, till they were sundered and Don was free!

She dropped the knife, sank to the floor unconscious. But Don knew that somehow "Mary" had reasserted herself at the last moment.

He was free! For a moment the three men and the woman stared at him, spellbound. Then with a smothered oath, Purvis leaped for his desk and began tugging at a drawer. Pugh leaped forward, fists flailing. Don's right shot out and caught him a crack on the jaw that dropped him like a log.

Emerson had the knife. He struck as he sprang, and the point of the blade ripped Don's coat. Don grasped his opponent's wrist and fought madly for possession of the weapon. From the corner of his eye, he saw Purvis pulling a revolver from a drawer of the table. He had just two seconds.

He made the best use of them. He wrenched the knife away and struck upward with all his strength. A shriek of agony broke from Emerson's lips as he toppled, sliced almost to backbone and midriff by the razor-edge. As he fell, Pugh picked himself up and came running in groggily, fists flailing wildly.

In the same instant Purvis's panic-shaken hand discharged the revolver. Pugh stumbled, tried to scream, and dropped over the dying Emerson, blood welling to a red froth at his lips. Purvis's bullet, aimed at Don, had pierced Pugh's heart and lung.

It was a scene of horror: the unconscious girl; the screaming nurse cowering terror stricken against the wall; Purvis, with the revolver describing wide circles as his hand shook like a palsied man's; and the two men on the

(Continued on page 123)

THE ASTOUNDING ADVENTURES OF
OLGA MESMER

OLGA, ROD and SHAG run abruptly from the scene of the revolt of the Sitnaltans in an effort to find a long-hidden electric gun.

Her X-ray eyes enable OLGA to find the crypt in which it has been stored, and they find the outfit complete, except for a necessary ground cable. Shag offers to use his body for the contact.

But while these three assemble the ray-gun, Ombo and his rebels are gaining ground.

— an eerie silence sweeps the ranks of Ombo's men: "Quietus!" —

THE GIRL WITH THE X-RAY EYES

"Magic Machine"

Aiming cautiously, Olga snipes at the outline of Ombo and paralyzes him also.

Rod revives Queen Margot with the water which renews her reign each year.

YOU'VE ALL BEEN SO GOOD! IS OLGA SAFE? WHERE IS SHAG?

SHAG IS THE MOST LOYAL SERVANT A QUEEN EVER HAD, YOUR HIGHNESS,- CAN'T HE BE PUT OUT OF HIS MISERY?

BUT HOW? OH SHAG, MY LOVE!

OUR PRINCE CAN DO IT, MY QUEEN!

REAL SLEEP! MY QUEEN - LET ME DIE! MARGOT! I HAVE LOVE, PROTECT YOU THIRTY THOUSAND YEAR! I CANNOT HEAL, I CANNOT DIE. HAVE PRINCE DRAW THE EVER-LIFE FROM OUT MY HEART! HE CAN GIVE IT TO YOUR DAUGHTER.- SO SHE WILL NOT DIE!

SHAG, I HAVE ALWAYS LOVED YOU! DO YOU REALLY WANT TO DIE FOR OLGA? MY SAINT!

DEALER IN DEATH

IT WAS damnably queer, he thought as he went slinking through the night, that he should have this feeling of fear. The sensation was new to him; he could not fathom it.

He who dealt in wholesale death; who had hanged more than half-a-hundred men and women, callously indifferent to their innocence or guilt—why should he tremble now? A public hangman should be above fear, he tried to tell himself. And yet—he was afraid.

No ghosts of executed victims troubled his conscience, for he possessed no conscience. Nor did he repent his past misdeeds, black though they were. In faith, he thought sardonically, it was he

By ROBERT LESLIE BELLEM

It was a powerful, demon brew the gypsy girl mixed for the hangman, and he thought it would bring the girl he loved back from death . . . even after he had hanged her. Little did he realize the depth of vengeance in a Romany heart

His thumbs closed upon her windpipe. She gasped, "I expected this, hangman."

himself who should long ago have danced a macabre rigadoon on the gibbet at Gallows Hill, instead of some of those hapless fools whom he had swung into Eternity. But he was far too smart for such an inglorious end; too clever and crafty.

No; his gruesome profession bothered him not at all. On the contrary, he took a sort of saturnine pleasure from his method of livelihood. His bloated paunch rumbled with unhallowed mirth when he considered his own cleverness. Who else in all medieval England could have contrived such a way of attaining wealth? There was satanic perfection in it. First he would secretly denounce some unsuspecting fool with an accusation of witchcraft or sorcery; for every victim thus unearthed and convicted, he received twenty golden crowns. And twenty more when he hanged the man or woman in question. . . .

TONIGHT, however, he knew the meaning of fear. It was spawned of the visit he was planning; his visit to Lyala, the gypsy girl. Odd, how he dreaded the forthcoming meeting; yet call on Lyala he must—for she was the only one who might help him in this, his hour of need.

A curiously sinister figure in the long black cloak that draped his squat, ape-like frame, he shambled onward through the midnight's intense blackness. His mouth tasted peculiarly coppery and metallic; his inflamed brain burned with heated thoughts of a certain golden haired maiden who lay condemned to death back in London Tower.

He must see that glorious wench again before she died, he whispered savagely to himself. Regardless of the consequences, he must woo her, win her, even if only for an hour; no matter what the price he might have to pay for gypsy Lyala's aid. Once and only once had he laid eyes on the maiden; yet her remembered blonde beauty haunted him with prickling, all-consuming fire. . . .

He reached Lyala's thatched hovel.

Within, a fire flickered on the open hearth, filling the rude hut's single room with dancing demons of light. To an unglazed window the hangman affixed his gaze. "By'r Lady!" he whispered in sharp amazement.

The gypsy girl was preparing to retire; had removed her outer garb and her coarse undershift. Clad now in little but a bright crimson loincloth, she stood before the fire as she ran a comb through the long black tresses which cascaded to her slender waist, partially draping the tawny gleaming cones of her young breast.

Her movements were sleekly feline. Ripples of smooth symmetry danced along her arms as she raised them to her raven locks; her breasts were drawn upward to tempting firmness under the semi-revealing strands of her flowing hair. Her skin was smoothly golden, her form slender and wholly feminine. Long and tapered and shapely were her brown legs; like a masterpiece of the sculptor's art her thighs. And her face possessed a weird, wild beauty matched by the dark glow in her sombre eyes; there was a hint of tragedy in the set of her sullen, sensuous mouth. . . .

For a long moment he watched her, while a scheme hatched in his cunning brain. Then he went to the hovel's door and entered without knocking.

LYALA whirled to face him; her palms dropped to shield her bosom. "How darest thou—!" she exclaimed. Then her eyes widened as he removed his cloak and revealed his identity. *"The hangman!"* her lips formed the soundless words.

His smile was unpleasantly like a sneer. "So you know me, do you, wench?"

Bitterness entered her tone. "I would know thee anywhere. Didst thou not hang my mother for witchcraft, six months agone?"

He had not forgotten. This was one of the factors he must overcome ere he win Lyala's aid in his enterprise. "Aye," he nodded with feigned remorse. "Hang her I did. But 'twas no fault of mine, I trow. I did but carry out my duty according to law. I had no hand in her denouncing and her conviction," he lied glibly.

Then through narrowed eyes he studied the effect of his words; wondered if Lyala would believe. Because in truth he had secretly caused the arrest of her mother— an arrest which had netted him the usual fee in gold.

The gypsy maid met his gaze, her own eyes shadowed and enigmatic. Then, slowly, she smiled. "Thou art right, hangman. Innocent wert thou of complicity in my mother's fate." She leaned forward to cast more faggots on the dying fire; the movement caused her midnight hair to cascade away from her breasts, so that his eyes could not help but glimpse those enticing charms of their full, feminine glory. Then she spoke again. "Why hast thou come here tonight?"

He put his hastily-conceived plan into motion. Nor was it any great task to summon an esurient expression to his piggish eyes. The challenge of her gaceful young body was enough to charge his blood with the heat of expectation —something completely unfeigned. "I came to speak to you of a certain matter," he said. "But having seen your beauty, that matter is now forgotten. . . ."

Her crimson lips parted to display even, sharp white teeth. Her slim hips weaved subtly as she took a step toward him. "Thy meaning is not clear, hangman," she whispered. But her smile belied her words. She knew what he meant, he felt sure. She could not possibly misunderstand the avidity with which his gaze licked over her. . . .

SHE reclined lazily upon her couch of rushes; made room for him to perch his squat form beside her. Through the dark waterfall of her hair he could again glimpse the warm beauty of her tawny bosom; and a churning seethe of sensation swirled through his veins. "Thou art more tempting than the devil himself!" he spoke softly.

Her laughter was tinkling and brittle. "Art not afraid that I have bewitched thee, hangman?"

"Bewitched I am," he agreed

hotly. "But not by any black sorcery. My enchantment comes of feasting my vision upon thy golden skin, thy perfect form." He reached forth to stroke her blue-black tresses, artfully contriving to dislodge partly the long strands which concealed her lustrous bosom.

Higher mounted his feelings as she did not parry the deft caress. He could see throbs of quivering movement dancing across sleek flesh, the rounded symmetry of her undraped thighs seeped into his blood. He ran his thick fingers over her shoulders, sensing the velvety smoothness of her skin. He began to breathe with wheezing difficulty.

And then she laughed—and locked her arms around his neck. Her red mouth parted before his lips. She fused herself to his apish body and clung.

Her kiss seemed to draw out his very soul; seemd to reach into his veins with a thousand red-hot needles. For some inexplicable reason he recoiled in horror—in fear. The suddenness of that fear was like the bursting of a black tropical storm.

Lyala drew away from him, released him. "So you lied to me, after all!"

"I—I—"

"Thou hast no real love for me."

He saw his schemes crumbling. "Not so, gypsy wench. But—but —I—"

Her eyes were clouded. "Thy actions were a sham. It was a trick to gain some other favor of me."

How could she read his mind so thoroughly? His fear rose up in his thick throat, choked him. "Thou art mistaken!" he mumbled.

"No; thy kiss told me . . . everything." She arose from the bed of rushes, slipped into her coarse shift and tossed more faggots upon the embers on the hearth. When she faced him again, she was utterly calm. "It matters not, hangman. Name the thing you wish; perhaps I can help you after all. If you pay me gold," she added with typical Romany avarice.

He took heart. From the pouch at his bloated waist he extracted twenty yellow coins; a secret amusement rippled through him when he remembered how he had gained those golden pieces. They were the fee he had earned by denouncing Lyala's gypsy mother as a witch. . . .

"Twenty crowns," he said softly. "All for you, wench—if you can help me."

She accepted the clinking coins. "What task is this?"

HE lowered his voice. "In London Tower lies a certain maid, by name Helen. Denounced was she for conspiring against the King, and now she must die—tomorrow."

"Didst thou denounce her, hangman?" Lyala whispered evenly.

"By'r Lady, no!" he protested vehemently—and truthfully, for once. Because the blonde maid, Helen, was in chains through no act of his. Some other informer had been at the bottom of that particular arrest.

"And this maid hangs on the morrow? At your hands?"

He nodded. "At my hands!" he

groaned. "I must kill the one I love...!" His greasy lips writhed. "It cannot be! I must save her. And you shall help me, gypsy! You must!"

Lyala smiled. "It can be done, methinks. Do thou sit down and wait, hangman, while I prepare a brew...."

He watched as she added new fuel to her fire and placed a black pot thereon. Fascinated, he saw her capture a sleeping chicken, chop off its head, and allow the hot blood to flow into the cauldron.

"You are the hangman," she moaned, "you have come for me."

To the bubbling black mess she added certain seething powders, the dried eyes of an owl, the skin of a toad, and certain other unmentionable ingredients. She stirred the mixture, mumbling incantations over it. . . .

In time the noxious broth simmered dry. A stench-cloud of smoke arose, filling the thatched hut with nauseous fumes. Lyala removed the pot and permitted it to cool, slowly. Then with a pewter ladle marked with cabalistic designs she scraped the burned dregs from the sides and bottom of the cauldron, carefully catching each charred flake in a hollow leaf from the stem of some odd plant the like of which the hangman had never before seen.

When the twisted spill was handed to him, he accepted it gingerly. "For what purpose is this, oh gypsy?" he demanded. There was a quaver in his voice that he seemed unable to control.

"Take it to thy condemned maid. Tell her to swallow it just before she is led to the gallows. Have no fears, sweet hangman; for the potency of the mixture will indeed triumph even over death itself."

"You—you mean—?"

"The one you love can be hanged upon thy gibbet, yet will she return to life on the magical seventh day after her burial. This I promise thee upon pain of forfeiture of my own life. Come ye back to me on the midnight of the seventh day from tomorrow. Then shall I help thee open thy maiden's grave and restore her to thy ardent arms."

A VAST, saturnine satisfaction filled him. Already his crafty brain was at work upon a new scheme. Were the authorities to learn of his plan to cheat the gibbet of a victim, he might find his own heels jigging on air while his neck strained against a hempen noose. . . . But the authorities would never learn, he promised himself. There would be nobody to tell them—except this gypsy wench, Lyala.

And as soon as the blonde maiden had been resurrected from her grave, Lyala would die. The hangman would see to that. His thick fingers tightened as if already closing about her tawny throat. . . .

But he was careful to conceal the murderous gleam in his porcine little eyes. He forced a smile of gratitude. "My thanks do I offer thee, gypsy. The favor is one I can never fully repay, methinks."

"It is nothing," she told him casually. "Good morrow to thee, hangman."

He went out.

And now by stealth he returned to the city, wending his way through thick swirling veils of fog toward London Tower. Entering that prison of the condemned, his presence went unnoticed—for was he not the hangman, with a perfect right to inspect the doomed ones whose lives he was to snuff out on Gallows Hill? Past nodding, sleepy guards he shambled; and at last he came to the cell where the fair-haired Helen lay helplessly chained.

By the light from a flare in the dank corridor, she was revealed in all her abject misery. She was crouched in a corner of her dungeon, her sole garment a cotton shift that thinly caressed the magnificent contours of her young body. Through the material could be seen the soft sleekness of her flesh, the lilting curves of her hips and swelling bosom. Her pallid face was ethereally beautiful; her long hair was like spun strands of mid-noon sunshine. The mere sight of her sent leaping surges of bestial yearning through the hangman's dark heart.

He unlocked the cell-door and strode into the chamber.

At his appearance the blonde girl sprang fearfully to her feet, her chains rattling rustily. "No—oh God—no—!" she whimpered.

He licked her with his eyes. "Now by'r Lady, what fear is this, sweet maid?"

"You are . . . the hangman . . . you have come to take me. . . !" she moaned.

SO she had recognized him! Perhaps, upon a time, she had seen him perform his gruesome duties —never realizing that one day she herself would be victim of his professional ministrations. He regretted her recognition, for he wanted her love—not her terror. "Be quiet, sweetling. I have not come to harm thee," he whispered unctuously.

Her azure eyes widened. "Then why are you here?"

Greedily his gaze devoured her soft loveliness. In some prior struggle her shift had been torn, so that the tatters barely concealed the gentle white slopes of her rounded bosom. And as she stood between him and the light, he could discern the sweet perfection of her legs; the moulded symmetry of her firm thighs. Never was any wom-an so gloriously made, he thought; never had any maid possessed such sheer perfection of figure. His palms tingled; sweat stood out on his forehead; every fiber of his being cried out with the need to crush her close, savor the delicious warmth of that glorious beauty. . . .

But he restrained his impulses for the time; he must work gently, he told himself, to win her confidence and her love. "I have come to save you from death," he answered her affrighted query.

"You—the hangman—save me from d-death?"

He nodded.

"But why, messire? Why?"

"Because . . . I am mad about you!" He had not intended so abrupt a declaration; but the words seemed to tumble in unbidden torrent from his oily lips. He stepped forward, seized her in his arms, crushed her in a simian embrace that constricted her chest and forced the gasping breath from her red lips.

He felt the cushioned flesh-softness of her upon his chest, firmly yielding and ecstatically thrilling. His finger-tips danced over her shoulders and her back, extracting every last iota of sensation from the contact. He mashed his mouth upon her lips; kissed her bestially, savagely.

At last she squirmed free, panting from the unexpected vigor of his embrace. "But—marry—how couldst ye love me, whom ye do not know?" she whispered faintly, recovering her breath.

"I saw thee once, when thou wert condemned to death. And since then I have dreamed of thee, waking and sleeping, until my body

aches with longing to hold thee—''
Once more he engulfed her in the
circle of his arms, crushing her
writhing lips with the slimy avidity
of his kiss.

A WAVE of sheer revulsion
seemed to sweep over her. She
clawed at him, fought him silently
and desperately. "Let me go!
Sooner would I die than permit
you to . . ." Her voice died away;
her demeanor suddenly changed.
"Forgive me, hangman. I—I am
distraught; I know not what I am
saying. How wilt thou save my
life?" Her smile was palpably
forced, her coquetry obviously as-
sumed.

He scowled, for he realized the
trend of her thoughts. She cared
not for him; she secretly felt revulsion for his advances. But in
her desperation she was willing to
pretend an ardor she did not feel
—if, in return, he would keep her
from the gallows. He sensed this;
knew it to be true; and for an
instant, black wrath churned in his
vast belly.

Because he wanted no unwilling
surrender on her part. He desired
her love—but it must be voluntar-
ily given. Yet how could he
achieve his desires, in the face of
her loathing?

Then he thought of Lyala, the
gypsy.

Yes; Lyala would know a way to
effect this consummation. She
would brew another broth, con-
coct a love-potion. . . . But he
must proceed with the utmost cau-
tion; he must act warily, so that
this sweet golden-haired maid
would not suspect his intent. He
forced an apologetic smile. "Be

of good faith, sweetling. I can per-
ceive that thou desirest none of my
kisses. If it be thus, so let it be.
Still will I fain save thee from
death."

"Ye—ye would help me, yet ask
no reward?"

"None other than thy thanks."

"Gladly would that be given,
hangman. But how—how can you
keep me from the gallows, since
I have been convicted of treason?"

He frowned. "That I cannot do.
Thou must hang, sweetling."

"Oh-h-h. . . !" Her pallor grew
more pronounced; her breasts
heaved with tumultuous panting—
a swift rise and fall of enticement
that filled the hangman with rip-
tides of fire.

But he held himself in check;
lowered his voice to a soothing
whisper. "Aye. Hang ye must; but
die ye need not."

"Methinks ye jest—!"

"By'r Lady, no!" He held forth
the twisted green-leaf spill. "Here
is a magic powder which thou'lt eat
just before thou'rt taken to the
gibbet. 'Tis a witch-brew that will
bring back breath of life to your
lovely body e'en though death shall
have claimed thee."

She was trembling as she took
the spill. "Thou w-wouldst not
give me so monstrous a lie, hangman?"

"God's truth I tell ye—or rather,
the devil's!" he answered. "Ye'll
eat the powder at dawn of the morrow? I have thy promise?"

"My sacred promise," she whispered fearfully.

Stifling his urge to kiss her, he
went forth from her dungeon.

And at the rise of the sun, that
next morning, he hanged her.

AS he adjusted the hood and the noose, he managed to touch her trembling flesh; as if by accident his fingers brushed across moulded, taut curves. The contact flooded him with dark seethings of emotion, so that he almost bungled the slipknot. God ... suppose the

didst thou follow my instructions?''

"I—I took the powder, hang-

By the light of the flare, he could see her ethereal beauty.

thing went wrong? Suppose the gypsy's hell-brew lacked potency? Suppose . . . suppose the fair-haired maid had not consumed the dose?

As he supported her upon the trap, he whispered: "Sweetling—

man," she answered faintly through the black hood that concealed her lovely features.

He drew a gasping breath, stepped back—and released the trap-mechanism. From the watching crowd came a rippling tide of catcalls as the blonde girl's body shot downward on a course sickeningly arrested by the sharp jerk of the rope. . . .

She dangled there, feebly kicking, until at last the final tremors subsided in her fair flesh; and she was cut down and pronounced dead; and she was buried in a shallow grave at the foot of Gallows Hill, within the edge of a dark and whispering grove of trees. . . .

AND now came seven days of torturing doubt for the hangman; days of wild misgivings and nights of fantastic dreams, peopled with leering ghost-shapes of innocents whom he had slain. Then, upon the midnight of the seventh day, he went once again to the hut of Lyala, the gypsy wench.

She was waiting for him, her dark eyes cloudily enigmatic and her sensuous lips twisted in a queer smile. "Ah, hangman!" she greeted him. "I have been expecting thee."

With brusqueness he attempted to hide the fears that coursed icily through his veins. "Let us waste no time!" he choked. "'Tis the night of my fair maid's resurrection. . . ."

"Aye, that it is, hangman. Thou art ready? Thou hast digging tools?"

He nodded. "But stay, gypsy. There is something else."

"And that?"

"This maid—she loves me not. I am repugnant to her. How then can I win her when she is revived? My feeling for her scalds me . . . and yet . . . I want no simulated ardor. . . ."

Lyala laughed, her sharp teeth catlike and white against the tawny gold of her features in the fireglow. "I have a love potion, oh hangman. A potion which will make you desirable in the maiden's eyes when she beholds you. But it will cost you a price."

"Gladly will I pay. How much? Where is this brew? Fetch it—and swiftly!"

She narrowed her eyes. "Twenty pieces of gold."

Once more a secret amusement seized him. Already he had paid her twenty golden coins—the coins he had earned by falsely denouncing Lyala's mother as a witch. Now he would tender twenty more; and that would be the sum he had been given for hanging the old woman on Gallows Hill. He smothered his monstrous amusement that the daughter should now receive the coins he had earned by that killing. . . .

When Lyala had been paid, she produced a tiny phial. "Drink!" she commanded.

He obeyed. The stuff was oily, tasteless; he felt no change in himself as it spread through the cavernous reaches of his belly. Yet he knew now that his love would be invincible. A mighty egotism seeped into his consciousness. "Let us be gone!" he growled.

The gypsy wench clung to his arm, and together they slipped into the night.

They came at last to that unmarked grave under the trees; and at once they set to work, digging into the moist earth. When the shallow oblong hole had been opened, the hangman laid avaricious hands on the cheap board coffin; hauled it to the surface. He pried open the lid.

"Sweetling—!" he whispered.

THE golden-haired Helen lay in the calm repose of apparent death; nor did her eyelids flutter when he spoke. He slid his apish arms under her, lifting her from the rude casket. At first her flesh felt cold, clammy, oysterish . . . Then he seemed to notice a faint pulsation at her blue-bruised throat, where his noose had bitten into her white flesh. And warmth seemed to be stealing into her veins; he could feel it as he touched her and caressed her. . . .

. . . He saw her blue eyes staring up at him. . . .

She was alive! Now he was whelmed with dark ecstasy and churning anticipation. He lowered his mouth to her lips, planting a greedy kiss there. He felt her body stirring in his embrace. . . .

But first he had another task to perform. The gypsy wench was standing nearby, watching with sardonic amusement. She must be slain, else some day she inform the authorities of what he had done. He leaped to his feet, sprang at Lyala and wrapped his muscular fingers about her neck.

Her smile mocked him. "I expected this, hangman . . !" she gasped.

His thumbs closed on her windpipe. He throttled her until she no longer breathed; until he could feel no heartbeats when he placed his calloused palm against the soft flesh of her breast. He lowered her to the ground and kicked at her, viciously. "Thy tongue is forever stilled now, oh Lyala!" he chuckled.

And he returned to the golden-haired girl; took her in his arms again.

At first she was passive as he bruised her lips with eager beast-kisses. But gradually he felt a stirring in her flesh; felt her bosom growing taut against his chest. "Sweetling!" he panted, running thick fingers through the spun-sunshine masses of her hair. "Beloved —flower of beauty—fruit of loveliness—!"

What was her whispered answer, that he could scarcely hear? A term of endearment, surely! For were her lips not moistly parted upon his mouth? Were her white arms not locked about his neck there by the opened grave from which he had saved her?

His white-hot emotions burgeoned into flame-blossoms of longing. He stormed more kisses upon the blonde girl; rained them upon her eyes, her mouth and the hollow of her throat. He tore at her cheap white shroud, so that he could feast his gaze on the curving perfection of her creamy flesh; so that he could savor the pearly sleekness of her hips and her thighs. . . .

And then—

What sound was that?

TO his dull senses, it came again: a croaking, whispered ghost of

(Continued on page 94)

By ROSS FLYNN

SMALL EVIL

I WANTED it the first time I saw it! I wanted it more than anything, I had ever seen before, with an even deeper craving than I had felt for the superb, arrogant young beauty of old Keneidos's daughter, Luciella. And God knows I had yearned for her through many a lonely hour, the vision of her lush, exotic loveliness shimmering as in a dream before me until I had to force my

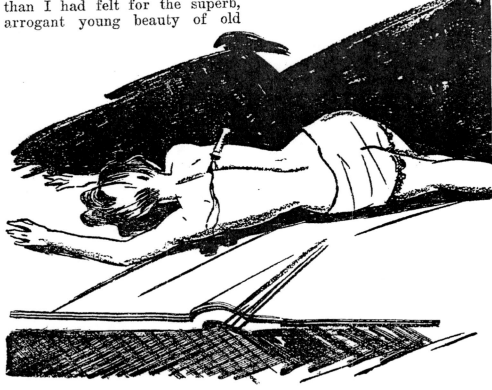

Joan's arm was around me. On the
floor was the still figure of Luciella.

It was a thing of golden provocative beauty, a sleek
little figurine of lifeless stone . . . but in it was hell
incarnate, the evil of the ages. And it took blood to
keep the fires of life burning

nails into my palms to keep from crushing her warm young beauty in my arms.

This thing wrapped the same mood around me, but with an even deeper fascination that was so uncanny I could not help but fear it. Yes, I feared it—and knew that I had to have it for my own.

It seems mad, perhaps, to confess such thoughts about a statuette. For it was nothing more than that: a figurine, perhaps six inches high, its smooth surface glowing with the silky sheen of porcelain, although it was made of some other substance, the like of which I had never seen before.

I came across it in Keneidos's murky den in the basement. What sort of business he did in that place I had never been able to learn, if indeed he had a business at all. Shutters were always closed over its barred windows; inside was a hushed gloom and a jumble of strange objects: antiques, relics, curios from all over the world. God knows how he amassed that pile, or how he came to live his life of a virtual recluse in this buried back street of the great city—or how the lithe provocative beauty of Luciella ever was spawned by his twisted old body.

I had two rooms on the second floor of the house. I had taken them because they were cheap, and perhaps (although I didn't admit it to myself) because I'd caught a glimpse of Luciella.

Sometimes I'd see her when I came home at night from my work. She'd be standing in the dim hall, the curves of her figure outlined in a breathtaking silhouette of arrogantly outthrust breasts, richly curved hips and thighs. Several times she brushed against me as I passed her to go up the stairs. Sometimes I thought she deliberately allowed her soft body to touch mine, lightly, to torment me with the very nearness of her.

It would have been all to easy to grasp her, flatten the whole pliant length of her against me, bury my thirsty lips in the moist, savage crimson of her mouth—all too easy! But there was Joan: she was coming to me soon, and we were to be married. Only by filling my mind with the great promise of her love was I able to resist the allure of Luciella's lithe body and half-mocking, lash-veiled eyes.

But she taunted me in my dreams, Keneidos's daughter, and she put me through a very hell of anguish the one night she appeared in my room. It was late; I was reading, was getting sleepy . . . until she came in. She wore, I remember, a robe of crimson silk, that clung tightly to her soft curves; her long hair tumbled in a gleaming torrent down her back; her full lips were parted over flashing white teeth in a seductive smile.

She moved toward me with a languorous grace as I got up from my chair, and I felt my pulse quicken and my arms ache to hold her as she moved one firm, slim leg forward so that it brushed against mine, and let the flaming robe loosen a trifle. A sleek creamy curve appeared at the vee of her robe, and I stared at the tawny skin of her breast through misted eyes. She knew how I felt about her, alright! Her supple body swayed—and she laughed as I wrenched my head away. In a harsh, cracked voice I told her to go. I waited, biting my lip until the blood came, while she backed away, taunting me with the sinuous movements of her body, with that low, mocking laugh. . . .

I SHOULD have known; I should have left that silent brooding house. That night, as I lay staring into the hot darkness, I determined to do so, knowing that if I did not go I would lose forever the shining glory of Joan's love.

But when I went down into the basement the next day to tell Keneidos, I saw the statuette— and I was lost!

It swept all other thoughts from my head. It stood there proudly by itself on a shelf in Keneidos's hushed, shadowy den; light from the one dim bulb fell softly on it, and its weird beauty held me breathless.

It was of a warm golden hue, making it seem somehow to pulse with life, as if it were human skin that stretched tautly over the swelling mounds of the perfectly carved breasts, the flat, smooth stomach, the long flanks and delicately chiseled legs. The face was of unearthly beauty, the eyes wide and slanting, the cheeks cast in high, exotic planes. Golden-bronze hair curled in a rippling mass around the head. Formed with divine craftsmanship, it was the tiny figure of a woman, standing with arms held high as if in a gesture of supreme exaltation, or perhaps sacrifice—the body enticingly curved, the legs bent slightly. Dancing girl—priestess? I did not know, did not care! All I knew was

that the sight of it bred in me such a passion to own it, to have it for my very own, that I felt weak and shaken.

I called for Keneidos, but he did not answer. Coming closer, I slowly stroked the figurine, and the tips of my fingers tingled as I did so, as if it were warm living flesh they felt. I could not explain the spell that had enwrapped me. It commanded me, and I was helpless in its grip!

There was a sound behind me that cut the uncanny tension. I turned to find Luciella standing close to me, her mocking eyes smiling up at me. My face flushed as I thought that she must have seen me fondling the statuette; I muttered to her to tell her father that I wished to see him that night, and rushed out of the place.

Yes, I had to see him. But no longer to tell him that I was moving. There was a different reason now.

IT GREW in me all day, the weird passion. It left me good for nothing else; my eyes were unseeing, my movements and speech clumsy and slow. The little figure danced before me, no longer motionless, but vibrant with life: the sensuously weaving body of a golden-skinned woman, hips swaying in a rhythmic, intoxicating pattern, marble breasts dancing, scarlet flower of mouth parted invitingly. The vision was very real. There were shadows around her, and behind her rose a looming mass of darkness. From somewhere above, a beam of sparkling ruddy light showered whorling motes of flame over her writhing, curving body, and now again great creeping forms seemed to move across it, smothering the livid glow, painting the whole strange scene in blackness. . . .

A presentiment of unholy evil grew in my fevered brain even as my whole being yearned. Passion and fear: an ungodly mixture. A hundred times I swore I would not enter that shrouded den again; as twilight softened the city I went into a bar, downed brandy after brandy, trying to deaden my senses to the call, but I had lost control; my legs would not obey. Like a drugged thing I stumbled through the night toward my enchantress.

Keneidos found me standing before the tiny form, my avid fingers smoothing over the swelling curves. "You like her, eh?" he said, pushing his bony, leering face close to mine; the bottomless pits of his eyes peering at me.

"Her?" I stammered. "Oh—oh yes! Where did she—where did it come from? What is it?"

He let out the broken exhalation that was his mirthless laugh. "Who knows? She is old, very old; perhaps as old as this earth we stand on. There are many legends about her. . . . I have heard she is a priestess of the dark place that our forefathers once feared and worshiped, and that this little form is but the shell she rests in until she sees one whom she loves. Then, I have heard, she lives again. . . . But that, of course"—he laughed again, chillingly, peering at me suddenly—"is but a tale made for an old wife's telling. . . . You want her?"

"I—want her?" My heart was in my throat. "Yes," I choked.

The stained stubs of his teeth showed in a leering smile. "All right," he said. "You like her so much, you keep her. Yes, you keep her for a while."

I DID not wait for more. I did not question the old man's generosity; I was afraid he would think better of it. I mumbled something and grasped the statuette. I held it tightly against my chest as I found my way to the stairs and climbed up to my room.

I closed the door. I was breathless with anticipation of I knew not what, like a young lover going to his first rendezvous—skin moist with cold sweat, pulse hammering. I turned on only one light, in the far corner of the room. I swept a vase off a small table, and it fell to the floor with a splintering crash. I do not think I was aware of the sound.

I placed the sleek golden figure on the table almost reverently and crouched before it. I don't know how long I remained there, while tiny cat-feet seemed to patter up and down my spine. My eyes were misty and I groaned in an agony of hopeless love and utter enthrallment.

The old house was very silent. Again I felt the unknown fear, the clammy forewarning of some primitive, buried sense that now was quivering and alive in my mind. I stumbled back and fell heavily on the bed. I pressed my hands to my whirling head—and stared through a rising tide of darkness at the witchlike thing on the table. *It was alive!*

Yes, alive! Not a figure of stone, cold and inanimate; a woman,

The two girls were fighting with pantherish fury.

warm and breathing, beautiful, desirable—and full-sized! I do not know how it happened; I only know that she was there, the living image of a statuette that had stood on a table, a tiny thing that had grown magically into this gorgeous flower of beauty.

The table was gone; yes, everything else was gone; this was a new world of crowding shadows and weird crooning sounds; of a column of leaping phosphorescent light that streamed down from awful, unimaginable heights and bathed in shimmering color the golden skin, the firmly outthrust bosom, the velvet hips and narrow waist and lithe, curving body of a woman who danced before her god. . . .

This was the vision I had had! The exact scene, whispering of unearthly things, of old evil, of a place of eternal darkness. There was the towering black mass, and dimly now I could see it for what it was. And it was hideous. It was all man's fear and horror and night-terror carved into reality. It was the black god, monstrous and all-powerful. It was the thing that spoke in the silence of the moonless night, the first primeval fear, the devourer, the unclean.

The woman danced before it in savage ecstasy, and the far-off wailing that brought a cold animal fear to my heart shuddered on the heavy air.

I could not move! It was as if invisible bands held my cowering body. I was no longer a man of the bright clean modern world; I was a witless dumb thing, crouching in naked fear before an ageless evil. The unremembered past, before man first found fire, lived around me.

THE dancer spun in a final frenzied whirl. She halted, her golden arms flung high above the bronze torrent of her hair, her uptilted breasts trembling, her flat, smooth stomach heaving. And then she turned slowly, and her lash-shrouded eyes fell lower—and gazed full into mine.

She smiled. Her lips were a moist scarlet gash over a row of flashing white teeth. Her hips swayed a little; the tawny breasts quivered. Her arms dropped slowly, and her veiled smile seemed to suggest the dark depths of passion. Then with a sudden swift movement that set her breasts dancing madly she flung forward into my arms.

A roaring tide lashed through my veins, sweeping that cold primeval dread of the unknown from me. She was close to me: that was all I knew in that mad moment. An intoxicating fragrance was in my nostrils, and moist full lips were crushed against mine. The insistent pressure of that perfect form was heavy upon my chest and I could feel the whole throbbing length of her against me. My arms lashed around her, moulding her to me, my hands roving over the velvet skin of her back, caressing the warm quivering flesh while our lips clung hungrily; the savage pressure of the embrace bruising the warm deep curve of her mouth. . . .

Ages might have whirled by me then—ages that passed like seconds. I remember a thousand shades of emotion sweeping through me—sudden cold fear, and love again, and horror of what lurked in the darkness surrounding us—and even horror of the lithe golden body; of the burning lips and white sharp teeth.

But the next thing I was vividly conscious of was the thin needle-pointed blade that suddenly was gleaming in her hand.

Sinuous, pliant as a snake, she curved against me. Her lips were red as heart's blood, her smile evil and secret, and her voice was murmuring in my ear. It was promising me an eternity of delights unknown to man, of ecstasies not of this world. But to gain them I must join myself with her, bind us together—I must let her drink of the life that ran in my veins; and then the great force that dwelt in the eternal darkness would give me the immortality that was hers, would lock me to her forever.

She was pressing close to me, her smooth hands stroking my cheeks. And the blade was at my wrist. There was a sudden swift stab of pain, then darkly gleaming blood spouted free. A delicious drowsiness crept over me—and her eager lips closed over my wrist. . . .

And then I knew no more.

I WOKE to blinding pain, and sunlight streaming into my eyes.

Full consciousness slowly returned to me. I was lying on the floor. For a few seconds I did not remember, then it all came burning into my brain. I started up suddenly, staring around me, half expecting to see that looming monstrous figure I had glimpsed in the weird darkness, and the golden body that writhed and curved before it and came with hungry lips toward me. . . .

But there was nothing—nothing save the familiar drab outlines of my room—and the fragments of a splintered vase on the floor and a tiny statuette on the table.

I stumbled over to it. I picked it up in my trembling hands and held it close to my eyes. It was the same: a thing of golden provocative beauty, a sleek little figure of lifeless stone, with arms held high and smooth hips slightly twisted, graceful legs half-bent—cold, inanimate!

My head was splitting, the room whirling around me. I staggered to a chair. A dream, was that all? I brushed one hand over my sweat-dewed brow. My eyes fell on the wrist, and I felt a shock go through me.

An angry line of red marked it. It had been cut by a keen blade. And those purple marks—clearly, they had been left by teeth, by the teeth of a woman!

I CANNOT remember what I did the rest of that day. I know that I did not stay in the silent house; yet I did not go to my office. I have a vague recollection of roaming the streets, of standing now and again at a bar, drinking. I was not sane; my mind was a confused, swirling torrent of a thousand evil things. Cold reason must have come to the surface more than once, for I remember telling myself that I must leave, that not only must I never return to the house, to the room, to the statuette, but that, to make certain, I must leave the city. But how could reason stand against that other—and fearful—urge, that came from searing remembrance of a lithe body crushed to mine, of moist scarlet lips and soft breasts and unholy ecstasy? It could not! Leave? Not return to the room? It would have been easier to kill myself.

Yes, I thought of Joan, and I longed for the pure beauty of her, as a prisoner longs for the freedom of the sunlit world beyond his

(Continued on page 92)

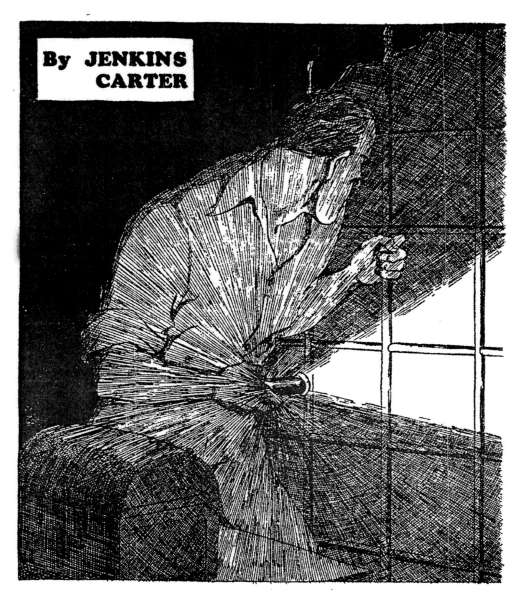

By JENKINS CARTER

THE VAULT

He had gone there for peace and quiet. He found terror, a mysterious terror, lightened only by a succession of beautiful women

THE place was exactly what Andrew Scribner wanted: an old rambling farmhouse miles from any big city, where he could work in solitude.

Yet when he drove up to it that morning, something was wrong. The old house frightened him. Its shaded win-

"You should have known," she said, "that there is nothing precious in money."

dows, glinting in the sun, were like beady eyes in the head of a huge beast, and the eerie silence that surrounded it was depressing.

Parking his car by the gate, he got out and stood there a while, trying to put a name to the strange fear that gripped him. Then, frowning at his own uneasiness, he yanked his suitcase from the car and strode up the weed-grown walk.

The ancient veranda steps creaked under his weight. With the key old Tom-kinson had given him, he unlocked the door.

It was murky and dank beyond that termite-eaten threshold, and for no good reason except that the place frightened him, he entered on tiptoe, left the door open behind him. His suitcase he dropped in the hall, and went prowling through the big, high-ceilinged rooms, raising tattered shades so that the sun might filter in through grimy windows.

Then he heard the scream.

It was so laden with terror that he

stiffened, clenched his hands and stood trembling. Short hairs bristled at the nape of his neck and he could feel his face changing shape as the muscles convulsed.

The scream came again, muffled by the carpeted floor beneath him. Eyes wide, he whirled about and strode back to the hall.

The stairs that led from the kitchen to the cellar were narrow and steep, and when he lurched down them his hands were outthrust, one gripping the rickety rail, the other pawing the concrete wall. His big body was bathed in sweat when he reached the bottom. His arms were hooked out in front of him.

HE SAW the girl before he had taken a dozen steps from the foot of the staircase.

She stood with her back against the far wall, staring at him. Light from a cobweb-covered window slanted down across her, exaggerating the wideness of her eyes, the lines of terror in her young face. Had she been less paralyzed by fear, she might have seized the spade that leaned against the wall beside her, and used it as a weapon.

She knew how to use it as a spade, that was certain, for one end of the cellar was dug up, and obviously she had done the digging. But she did not move, did not even cry out, merely stared at him as if he were something returned from a grave to destroy her.

He caught her as she slumped to the floor. His fingers gently pushed the damp hair from her eyes, and he marveled at the pale, waxen beauty of her face. One powerful hand slid to the warm hollow of her back as he lifted her.

He strode back to the stairs. The bedrooms were on the second floor, and he was gasping for breath when he lowered the girl onto a big four-poster and leaned over her.

She was lovely indeed, this girl! Not more than twenty years old, she had a slim, fully matured body in which every curve was like soft, sensuous music. Her dress was a flimsy, cheap little thing of cotton, torn now by his efforts in carrying her.

Her white shoulders gleamed like polished ivory. Her throat was a soft, supple arch shadow-blended with the gentle hollow of her full young bosom. Dazedly he stared at her, drinking in her beauty. Then—"Who are you?" he demanded.

Her silence filled him with a strange yearning. How soft she was! How sweet, with her eyes half closed and her pale lips faintly quivering! The crudely sewn bit of cotton that cradled her breasts was almost no covering at all. Her torn dress gaped to reveal sleek, moulded thighs that would have delighted a sculptor. Vaguely he wondered why she had been digging in the cellar.

"Who are you?" he whispered again, and then, as if drawn by a magnet, his lips descended to hers.

Her breath was warm, intoxicating. Hungrily he drank it in, fused his mouth with hers while his fingers awkwardly played with the long, silky strands of her golden hair. In a moment she would wake . . .

SUDDENLY a scowl twisted across his face and he leaned back, jerked his head around to peer at the bedroom door. Downstairs someone was hammering on another door, and a shrill voice reached up to him.

"Is they anyone home here? Hey? Is they anyone to home?"

Andy Scribner's big body trembled as he pushed himself erect and stood facing the doorway. The voice came again, yelling up from below, and he paced slowly over the threshold, pulling the door shut behind him.

At the top of the stairs he halted, peered down, and saw her in the gloom of the hall. An old woman, leaning there on a stick, glancing this way and that as if in search of something. Scowling, he went down to her.

"What do you want?" he said curtly. "Who are you?"

She stared at him out of glittering little eyes in a wrinkled face. Not more than five feet tall, she was as old, or nearly as old, as the house itself.

"Seen the front door open," she said, "so I knocked and come on in. So you're the young man that rented this place, are ye? Well, I'm your nearest neighbor. Name's Aggie Bradley. I live up the road a piece, in the little shack with the two big elm trees afront of it."

"I told Mr. Tomkinson," Andy Scribner said, "that I didn't want any visitors."

"Humph! You are a queer one!"

"What do you want?"

"Want? Nothin', 'cept to say hello to ye. Lived here once myself, I did, and I was lonesome enough to make friends with the snakes and the hoptoads, even. Scared, too, most of the time, when I'd be hearin' them voices."

Andy Scribner narrowed his eyes at her and wondered if she were half crazy. The dress she wore was filthy and ragged, and covered almost nothing. He could see her withered flesh through the rents. Every place where her body should have curved, there was pathetic flatness or even a hollow. It was as if she had hammered herself with her fists while screaming at the moon.

"What voices?" he demanded hoarse-ly.

"You'll be hearin' 'em, mumblin' and whisperin' at ye. Don't think you won't." She wagged a bony hand at him as she retreated down the hall. "And you'll be grateful enough for company of *any* kind, 'fore long! You wait and see!"

He watched her, scowling, as she shuffled over the threshold. She was barefooted, he noticed. Then he shrugged his shoulders, paced after her and closed the door, turned again to the stairs.

Strange, how tired he felt. It was an effort even to walk. As if the old woman's beady eyes had drawn the strength out of his muscles. He had to grip the railing on the way upstairs, had to rest at the top. When he pushed open the bedroom door, he almost fell.

THE girl was sitting on the edge of the bed, her feet dangling to the floor, when he entered. She was frowning, as if wondering what had happened to her. She stared at him.

"W-who are you?" she whispered.

He put a hand on the bedpost to steady himself, while his widening eyes drank in her loveliness. "I'm Andy Scribner," he said quietly. "I found you downstairs and brought you up here." Strength was slowly returning and he felt better.

The girl was trying to hold her torn dress together, but was having little success. There was no fear in her eyes, though, as she gazed at him. She even smiled.

A dozen questions were on Andy's tongue but he left them unspoken. This was not the time for them. The girl was badly shaken up and needed reassuring. He walked over and sat beside her, put an arm around her.

"You're safe now," he said gently. "Please don't worry."

She was tired. She leaned against him, let her head rest on his shoulder, and the warmth and softness of her limp body were like low, soothing music in his veins.

"You haven't told me your name," Andy whispered.

She stirred sleepily and looked up at him. Her eyes were dark, deep, and her lovely lips were still highly colored from the pressure of his own. His gaze fastened on the sleek smoothness of her half-covered bosom, and he hardly heard her low-voiced reply to his question.

"I'm Rosemary Hammond," she said. "I live in the village."

"Then why did you come here?"

Was it his imagination, or did she hesitate before answering? Her mature young breasts seemed to swell with a suddenly drawn breath, yet her eyes continued to stare up into his, and her lips barely quivered. "I—I was looking for old Simeon's money," she said.

"Old Simeon?"

"Simeon Graves. He had this place before you took it. He died here, last year."

"But I understood that Mr. Tomkinson owned it."

"He doesn't, really. It belongs to old Simeon's sister, Aggie Bradley. But Aggie lets Mr. Tomkinson take care of it, and Tomkinson keeps whatever rent

he can get, in return for his trouble. Aggie, she doesn't need money. Simeon left her plenty."

Andy scowled. Somehow, the arrangement displeased him. There were too many persons involved, too many who might take it upon themselves to annoy him. If they found out he was a nationally known artist . . .

"And *you* were looking for Simeon's money?" he said. "You mean, that's why you were digging downstairs?"

THIS time it was not his imagination. Her face actually paled, her whole body stiffened and seemed to twitch away from his own. Looking into her eyes, he could have sworn that something vaguely

He saw the girl before he had taken a dozen steps.

terrible had suddenly come to life in their misty depths.

"Lots of people have looked for Simeon's money," she faltered. "He was a queer man, lived here all alone except once in a great while when Aggie used to come over to stay with him for a spell. In the village he used to talk a lot about his money. He had it, too. Used to get angry and throw handfuls of bills at people when they laughed at him. But when he died, no one could find it, and Aggie swore he didn't give anywhere near all of it to her."

"So people think it's still in the house here, eh?"

"Yes."

Andy Scribner sat there laughing, and liking the sound of his own gentle mirth, while the girl stared at him in bewilderment. "So my hideaway is a treasure house! Instead of being left alone, I'm to be plagued by droves of ambitious people with pickaxes and spades!"

"You—you came here to be alone?" the girl whispered.

He nodded, then found himself staring at her again, admiring the soft lustre of her wide eyes, the trim womanly curves of her. His arms trembled as he drew her closer. His tongue touched his lips, moistening them.

"I did want to be alone," he said huskily. "But now that I've met you, I . . . well, I hope you'll come back. Will you?"

She stood up, fumbling with the front of her dress. "I will," she said softly. "You know I will."

He sat staring at her as she departed.

THE rain began at four o'clock, and by six the old house was like a muttering, complaining monster with half a hundred eerie voices. Premature darkness made it necessary for Andy Scribner to light lamps even in the front living-room, and he sat there in an overstuffed chair, dismally trying to read.

The grotesque clock on the fireplace mantel ticked like a mechanical heart. Rain whispered at the shut windows. The floor creaked, the cracked ceiling muttered dolefully; even the chair in which he sat had an alien, frightening voice with which to torment him.

Then there were other voices.

They were vague and barely audible at first, and he put them down to his imagination, realizing that his nerves were on edge. But the voices persisted, came closer. The ceiling quivered to slow, grave-weary footsteps.

Andy Scribner clutched the arms of his chair, stared into the menacing gloom beyond the yellow murk of the lamps, and shuddered violently as icy fingers of fear caressed him. The chill beads of moisture clinging to his face and to the backs of his hands were not caused by the cold clamminess of the house, or by the storm outside.

Later he sneered at his own cowardice. The voices had gone. Common sense told him that what he had thought to be half-human whisperings had in reality been nothing more terrifying than faint echoes from the storm. This house was old. Like all old houses it was a vast beehive of rot-filled cracks and crevices—spawning-spots for eerie noises.

He read until eleven, then put out the lamps, climbed the stairs with a flashlight, and went to bed, thinking of Aggie Bradley and of the gorgeous creature who called herself Rosemary Hammond.

His dreams were of Rosemary, and they were pleasant. He held her in his arms; his wandering eyes watched the torn dress slip from her shoulders, baring flawless, milkwhite curves that flowed to the swelling mounds of her enticing breasts. Her lips whispered words of endearment, then parted, moist and red, for his hungry caress. His own lips murmured her name. "Rosemary. . . !"

THE answer was almost inaudible, yet he heard it, and it was no dream! "Here, my darling! Here I am!"

His eyes were open and he realized, vaguely at first, that she *was* in the room and that she was a creature of flesh and blood, no mere phantom of his dream! Her soft fingers, light as feathers, were smoothing back his hair. Her red mouth hung just above his own, smiling. He could taste the sweetness of her breath.

He sat up slowly, doubting his senses. His hands went out, trembling, to touch her, and encountered warm, living flesh as smooth as satin. There was no cheap cotton dress draped about her alluring body now! The thing she wore was cobweb thin, transparent—a kind of shroud. Every glorious curve of her mature young form showed through it. When she breathed, her rounded bosom swelled gently. She was a creature from some other world, some world of beauty and flaming emotions. Her voice was a sensuous caress that aroused dormant warmth within him.

"I had to come," she whispered. "I said I would, darling . . . and now . . ."

With more time to think things over, he might not have done what he did. But her presence, the exotic beauty of her, was a drug that lured his senses into a misty whirl of macabre music, of dim, mind-eating madness. Staggering to his feet, he dragged her close to him, twined his corded arms around her.

She did not resist, did not cry out, though the savagery of his embrace must have plunged knives of pain into her crushed breasts, and her quivering lips were flattened abruptly under his descending mouth. With an ardor that matched his own, she molded her slim body against his. Her soft hands caressed his face as he bent her to him. Low, wordless sounds of delight murmured from her throat.

He held her that way until the warmth of her threatened to overcome him and the burning pressure of her lips had sapped all strength from his own straining muscles. When he released her, she was reluctant to move away. Her fingers twined with his, and her mouth whispered words close to his throat.

"You must come with me," she said. "I have something to show you."

Dazed by what had happened, he would have granted anything she asked. When she drew him toward the door, he went willingly, rather than lose sight of her for an instant.

At the door she paused, said softly: "Bring your flashlight."

He followed her down the stairs, the flashlight in his hand casting a white pool ahead of her to guide her feet. They were bare, those feet, and seemed to know exactly where they were leading him, as if perhaps they had led others along the same mysterious way. Without hesitating, she paced along the downstairs hall to the kitchen, slid the bolt on the rear door and waited there for him to catch up with her.

"You have looked," she murmured, "for old Simeon's treasure?"

He shook his head. "No."

"In time you would have sought it," she said, "just as others have sought. In time, perhaps, the search would have driven you mad. I can save you from all that. Come!"

HEEDLESS of the chill drizzle outside, she stepped over the threshold and walked slowly ahead of him through weeds and grass that reached almost to her knees. It was the first time Andy Scribner had ventured beyond the rear doorway, and the wilderness disclosed by the flashlight's glare shocked him. The unkempt yard extended eerily into a vast, irregular wall of darkness where the clearing behind the house merged brokenly into deep woods.

Almost to the edge of the woods his guide led him, then stopped. When he reached her side, she pointed to a small slab of stone half hidden in the thick grass at her feet.

"Turn it over," she said.

He stared at her, frowning. An impulse struck him to play the flashlight's white pool over her face, but he refrained for fear of blinding her. Yet his mind, free now from the midst of madness induced by her loveliness, was filling with intuitions of impending peril.

Why was Rosemary acting so strangely about this idiotic business?

He forced himself to stoop, turn the stone. Then his eyes widened, breath hissed between his lips. Dropping abruptly to his knees, he used the palm of his hand to wipe away the dirt and crawling things that clung to the stone's under surface.

The flashlight showed him two rows of crudely carved words!

"You see?" the girl whispered.

Andy Scribner saw—and read. *"Cellar. S.W. Thirteen. Go, fool, if you must!"*

He stared up at her, said hoarsely: "What does it mean?"

"It is the key to Simeon's treasure," she declared softly. "Come!"

Andy straightened, scowling. A queer thrill crept through him. Treasure? Perhaps there *was* something worthwhile hidden in the old house, after all! Perhaps with Rosemary's help he would find it, and then . . .

But why the cryptic message, *"Go, fool, if you must!"* Why should those idiotic words be scratching like sharp-nailed talons at the shell of his mind, as if striving to warn him of some hideous danger?

Was the girl leading him into a trap?

He glanced at her again, while straightening from his crouch. The flashlight's glare laved the lower half of her glorious figure, revealing her slim, tapered legs, her lyrelike hips. She stood just a little apart from him, her face averted, as if she feared that he might flood her features with light. Was she essentially a creature of the night, a wanderer in darkness? Was she real?

He smothered a low laugh in his throat. Real? Her fiery kisses had been real enough, a little while ago! The ardent pressure of her pliant young body had been no illusion! And now she was holding out a hand, urging him to follow her again.

SHE led him back to the rear door, back through the kitchen and down the steep stairs to the cellar. The cryptic inscription was turning in his mind, and now he began to read sense into it. "*Cellar. S.W. Thirteen . . .*" Did that mean the southwest part of the cellar, thirteen paces from some wall?

He was almost correct. The girl led him silently to the southwest corner, carefully counted thirteen bricks up from the floor, thirteen over from the angle where the walls came together. "See?" she whispered, and lifted the brick from its resting place.

Andy aimed the light into the aperture, thrust his left arm in nearly to the elbow and grasped an iron ring. When he turned the ring, the whole wall trembled as if released. A section of it swung outward, and beyond that black aperture lay a vault of Stygian darkness so thick that even the slicing rays of the flash failed to make much impression.

"This," the girl whispered, "is Simeon's treasure room!"

Andy Scribner's eyes were wide. Breath hissed in his nostrils as he slowly paced forward. The fear that cursed like ice-water through his veins was a kind of drug that made every nerve-end supersensitive. He enjoyed being afraid. He felt light-headed, had trouble repressing the shout of triumph that welled up in his taut throat.

The girl did not follow him. Leaning in the doorway of the hidden room, she watched him, a lazy smile curving her lips as Andy advanced into the vault. But he was gripped by a strange, wild fever and did not notice.

The room was small. Earthen walls rose crookedly to a crude ceiling, and the floor was cold and damp under his feet.

"You see?" the girl whispered. "There are the directions."

The only doorway was the one through which he had entered. The only alien thing in the chamber was a rickety wooden table supporting an iron-bound chest red with rust.

Old Simeon's treasure hoard!

He strode toward it, the light dancing eerily ahead of him as his hands trembled with feverish anticipation. After his first quick glance at the walls and ceiling, he had eyes for nothing but the chest. He did not notice the broad rectangle of sheet-iron half covered by floor-dirt directly in front of the table.

His weight came down on it. He stiffened, felt the floor sag beneath him and lurched sideways. But the real horror of the room was not beneath that treacherous iron square. The real horror was behind him. Stunned by a harsh grating sound of steel on steel, mingled with the soft music of a woman's mocking laughter, he whirled. Whirled in time to see heavy iron bars drop with a metallic clang to block the doorway through which he had entered! His own footstep on the hidden mechanism had closed him in!

The flashlight fell from Andy Scribner's twitching fingers. Cold sweat oozed from the pores of his face, trickled down and stung his lips while he stood swaying. He took a faltering step toward the bars, stopped, bent over and retrieved the light. The girl was standing on the far side of the doorway, smiling at him.

Somehow there was nothing beautiful about her now. Her slim legs were the same, her flawless body had not changed, her lush breasts still swelled like living hummocks of white satin beneath the diaphanous film of her garment, but in her gleaming eyes lay a cruelty akin to madness. When Andy stumbled toward her, she retreated from the bars and uttered low laughter.

"You should have known," she mocked, "that money brings nothing but misery. Misery and death and horror!"

He licked his lips, jerked the flashlight higher and flooded her face with light. The eyes in his gaunt face narrowed. "Damn you!" he snarled. "I should have known! You're not Rosemary!"

"No . . . I'm not your Rosemary," she murmured.

Yet—yet the resemblance was so great that he could not make up his mind about her. Not Rosemary? God in heaven, then who was she? Some evil spirit of the night that could assume any desired shape, for the purpose of leading men to their doom?

He gripped one of the bars with his left hand, shook it. The woman laughed at his futile efforts. Slowly, still laughing, she retreated. While he stood there, numbed by what had happened, the wall swung shut with a dull, nerve-rending groan, completing his imprisonment. Then . . . silence.

FOR two hours, Andy Scribner raged at the bars, first shaking them with his hands, then reaching through them to claw at the solid mass of brick just beyond. The flashlight on the floor at his feet grew dim; the light in his death-cell was no longer white, but yellow.

At long last, drenched with sweat and hoarse from his continued yelling, he picked up the flash, limped to the other side of the room and sat down. Not until then did he remember the treasure-chest on the table.

A small oblong of paper was thumb-tacked to the lid of it. Grim words leered out at him. *"You have discovered the wealth of Simeon Graves, miserable mortal! For him it meant only unhappiness and loneliness. Yet he has the last laugh —because for you, fool, it means death!"*

The message ate like acid into his brain. A groan welled from his cracked lips. No longer had he any desire to open the chest. Even if it were filled with riches, what good would it do him?

He slumped to the floor again, sat there staring at the iron bars across the room. Too tired to assault the barrier again, he switched off the flashlight to preserve what was left of the half-drained batteries. The sudden rush of darkness frightened him, but he endured it, lay there pondering his fate.

What would it be? Starvation? Or would he go mad first, and die horribly while screaming at the four black walls that hemmed him in? Perhaps *she* would come again, to torment him with her vile laughter. Perhaps—

What was that?

He sat bolt upright, staring. A whisper had reached him through the barrier over there. His own name, softly spoken in a woman's voice! The torment again! But no; this was different. The voice was vibrant with the same terror that flowed in his own surging blood. The bars were groaning!

He swept the flashlight into his fist, thumbed the switch frantically. Then he was on his feet, staggering forward with a hoarse cry of thanksgiving. The bars were rising! The brick wall behind them was swinging open!

Trembling from head to foot, Andy Scribner swept into his arms the girl who stood there on the threshold. And this time no misgivings haunted him. This time he knew he was right!

She still wore the same ragged cotton dress, still had for him the same hungry kisses. Her slender body fused with his, warming him, driving out the damp chill which had taken possession of him. No weird creature of the night this time, but a flesh and blood Rosemary, come to release him from his dungeon of death!

"I—I watched you when you came here with that woman," she told him in a voice that was barely audible. "I was coming here to—to be with you—and I saw the two of you out back of the house. I watched through a cellar window while she led you downstairs, and I saw how you opened the vault . . ."

Andy shot a quick glance at the treasure-chest on the table. "That," he muttered, "is old Simeon Graves' hoard." But he did not move toward it. Later, perhaps, he and Rosemary would return for it, but now the essential thing was to get away from this unholy place before additional horrors overtook them. Rosemary had risked her life to release him.

FLASHLIGHT in hand, he pushed her over the threshold, steered her toward the stairs. She, too, was afraid of what might overtake them. The backglow of the flash showed her lovely face to be almost dead white, and he could feel her rounded bosom heaving against his encircling arm.

(Continued on page 100)

ROOM OF

In the room of magic he had found a doorway into the
Past. The curse that plagued him was hideous, beautiful!
Only through bloody murder could it lead him to love

By
JEROME
SEVERS
PERRY

neither of them in the long four years
intervening since their wedding. I'd
gone to South America—to forget. And
I had succeeded, almost.

But now I was back in my homeland,
summoned by Marcia's importunate
cablegram. And her sweet face, softly
aureoled with golden hair, reflected the
fear that had been contained in her message to me.

"Byrne—thank God you've come!"
she whispered as I stepped from the
train. Soaked by the steady autumn rain

MARCIA met me at the station.
Against the night's stormy
background, her pallor startled
me. She seemed haunted by some un-
voiced horror.

Marcia was my brother Clay's wife.
Once she had been my sweetheart. Then
she met Clay, fresh from college. He
won her away from me. I had seen

84

DREAMS

that hissed and spattered on the shed-less platform, she pressed herself into my arms.

She was still like a little girl; like a pink-and-white Dresden doll. Four years of marriage had not changed her. Her hips were boyishly slender; her firm bosom still domed and enticing. Every nubile nuance of her body was thrillingly limned by her wet silk frock.

She offered me her tremulous crimson lips.

The lonely years were swept away as I lowered my hungry mouth to hers.

The years of longing, when I had dreamed of her and yearned for her and bitterly realized that she was lost to me, were all erased in a flooding tumult of anticipation for this one kiss.

Our lips met.

A tingle of ecstasy cascaded through my veins; a shock of pleasurable sensa-

He swerved from the knife and heard a gurgling be-hind him.

tion filled me as her rounded little breasts pressed my chest. Then I released her, knowing that she belonged to my brother; knowing that she had chosen him in preference to me. I damned back the tides of desire that surged in my heart; fought against the magic of her will-destroying nearness.

"Why did you send me that cable, Marcia?" I asked her.

Once more her cheeks grew strangely pallid. "Oh, Byrne—Byrne—we need you! It's Clay. . . ."

"What about Clay? Is he ill?"

"Yes. N-no. I don't know how to answer you, Byrne. There's something horridly wrong with him. Not physical. It's as if a spell had been cast over him. A black, evil spell. It frightens me!"

She was leading me to her parked coupe. "Frightens you?" I said sharply. "In what way?"

"I—I think he's going to die!" she whimpered as we entered the little car. Then, before she started the motor, she squirmed around to face me. The movement drew the hem of her wet skirt up past her knees, affording me a glimpse of her tapered legs in the dashlight's glow; giving me a hint of white smooth flesh above dainty garters. . . . "Byrne, was there ever a strain of madness in your family?"

I STARTED to laugh at such a suggestion. Then I remembered my paternal grandfather, old Blake Lanier, who had built the solid mansion where Clay and Marcia now dwelt; who had founded the fortune which Clay and I had shared when our parents died.

Blake Lanier had been an Egyptologist; had been termed crazy by his neighbors, in the evening of his life. He had dabbled, they whispered, in dark sorceries; had held congress with the devil.

Of course that foolishness was based on the ignorant superstitions of country folk. True, my grandfather had been mildly eccentric. There was talk of secret rooms in his mansion; rooms where Egyptian treasure lay stored. But as boys, Clay nor I had never been able to discover such hidden chambers. And now, as a man grown, I refused to think of old Blake Lanier as insane.

I smiled at Marcia as she headed the coupe toward home. "The Lanier family was as sane as the next," I told her. "Surely you don't think Clay's mind is slipping?"

She shuddered. "You'll see for yourself," she promised me darkly.

The rain was not torrential; it was merely ceaseless, like a black enfoldment from the surly, low-hanging clouds. At last we stopped under the porte-cochere of the vast manse which Clay had accepted as his share of our mutual estate, leaving for me an equivalent amount in cash and securities. A warm nostalgia possessed me as I went to the front door of my old home. Here I had spent most of my life; here I had known happiness —and then heartbreak when I lost Marcia.

She opened the door.

At once I was repelled by an atmosphere—an aura—that seemed to leap at me hideously, on invisible wings. It was more than just a sensation; it was an *odor. . . !*

I attributed it to my imagination, and followed Marcia into the house.

She turned to me. "Clay's expecting you. He knows you're coming; knows I sent for you. You'll find him up in the old study, on the left wing of the second floor. You—you'll be careful, Byrne?" Her tone was fearful, and yet gentle; as if she desired no harm to come to me.

Once again my eyes devoured her

slender curves as revealed by the soaked, adhering silk. I wanted to crush her in my arms; to feel the throbbing firmness of her soft body against me; to taste the nectar of her parted lips, as I had done so many times in the dead past. But I controlled myself. "I'll be careful," I promised her. And I went upstairs, wondering what lay ahead that could possibly menace me.

The study door was ajar, and a dull light glowed within that oak-paneled room. I entered. "Clay!" the cry burst aghast from my lips.

MY BROTHER was sprawled in the depths of a leather chair; and his appearance struck horror into my heart. He had grown lean; almost cadaverous. His eyes were sunken into deep, gleaming hollows. His wasted cheeks clung to the framework of his facial bones; his hands were skinny, skeletal.

"Hello, Byrne," he greeted me sepulchrally. "I'm glad you're here at last. I need you—desperately." He made no move to arise.

"Clay!" I said again. "What's wrong with you, man? You're ill—!"

He smiled, and the effect was almost ghastly, so thin were his lips. "Ill? Yes. But none in the sense you mean. I'm bewitched—or else I'm going mad." He stirred feebly, like an old man. "It's up to you to find out which."

"I don't understand!" I whispered.

"You will when I've explained. Fill up your pipe while I talk. It'll take a long while to tell you everything." He shoved his tobacco-jar toward me.

I loaded one of the matched briars from my pocket. I waited.

Clay smiled again, horribly. "Grandfather Lanier's behind it. His damned delving in the tombs of the Pharaohs. It's a curse, I tell you. A hideous, beautiful curse!" He leaned toward me. "Byrne, I've discovered the old man's secret treasure-chamber. It's a room of magic! A doorway into the Past!"

How could a curse be both hideous and beautiful? What mortal can discover a doorway into the past? Clay's words were insane, incoherent, I thought. I began to realize that he actually had lost his reason. . . .

He seemed to sense my reaction. "Don't set me down as a madman yet, Byrne. Not until you've walked with me—through the Door. Then . . . if you don't see the same things I see . . . I'll know I've lost my mind. Are you ready, Byrne?"

Everything seemed vaguely unreal to me; distorted and formless, like a nightmare. "I'm ready," I told him.

He went to a paneled wall and pressed a secret spring. A whole section slid away, revealing a dark passageway. "Come," Clay whispered harshly.

I followed him into that dark space. The secret door closed behind us.

Then, directly before me, another door opened—*and I stared into brilliant sunlight!* Sunlight—though I knew the outer night was storm-swept and black!

NOR was I any longer under a roof. Above me, the azure sky was a cloudless vault shimmering in the noon sun. Endless vistas of fields and rolling hills stretched on every side, to the far horizons.

Clay chuckled at my elbow. "We've stepped into ancient Egypt!" he said. He studied my face. "It's true, isn't it? Tell me it's true, Byrne! Tell me I'm not crazy. . . !"

"It's true—or else we're both mad!" I grated as I tried to orient myself to this fantastic thing that had happened to me. I had walked from a dimly-lighted room—into the outdoors. I had stepped from night—into day. I felt lost, bewildered.

Clay gripped my wrist. "Come," he said. Beyond us lay a gentle hummock of brown earth, at a distance of perhaps a quarter-mile. There was an opening in the hill, leading down into an excavation. Toward this cavern I trudged, with my brother at my side. It seemed to take us hours before we reached our goal.

We stepped at last into that gloom-infested opening in the hill; and the dim infiltration of light from the entrance revealed the nature of the place. It was a burial-vault; a tomb.

Resting upon a marble block lay a golden sarcophagus of ancient Egyptian craftsmanship. I sensed a growing excitement in Clay's demeanor. "She sleeps there, Byrne—my Princess of Death . . . and of Love!" He raised his voice to a maniacal chant. "Waken, Princess of Dreams! Waken, for I hunger for your lips . . . ."

The lid of the sarcophagus was slowly rising. I felt my blood run cold. Out of that ancient coffin, a girl was gliding—

Her savage beauty stunned me. Dark was her long braided hair, like strands woven of the night sky. And dark were her glowing eyes that held a weird, sinister mockery in their depths. Mocking, too, were her crimson lips as they sensually smiled at my brother Clay. . . .

She emerged from the sarcophagus; and the symmetrical perfection of her body drew a gasping murmur from my throat. She was clad in flowing, filmy pleated robes of sheerest weave—through which I could discern the white smoothness of her flesh and the fluid curves of her form. Upon her milky breasts, round metal plates rested; a golden belt of metal encircled her supple waist, so that her draping robes flared downward away from lyric hips and columnar thighs.

Never have I seen such evil, such soul-destroying beauty. My brain reeled as I beheld her impossible perfection; my reason told me that this must be a horrid hallucination. Because her eyes and her smile and her lithe body were wholly demoniac. She was a creature of wickedness—of hell itself!

And my brother took her in his arms with a fierce, savage ardor.

Her tall, sinuous form yielded pliantly in his embrace. Her laughter was liquidly taunting—until he smothered it with his avid lips engulfing her mouth. One of the golden breast-plates became dislodged as he pulled her with him to a low stone bench; and through the thinness of her pleated robe I could see the erect mound of feminine charm that the metal had hitherto cupped and concealed. I closed my eyes against that dazzling vision; for already my own blood was flaming and leaping with wild, brutish longings. . . .

LONG moments later, when I dared look again, my brother was still embracing this weird, evil beauty; *but now he was paying the price of her kisses!*

She had her teeth in his throat. *She was drinking his blood!*

It sickened me. I started to rip out a harsh oath; started to leap at that feminine chimera whose lips sucked at Clay's very veins. But she drew back from him, and his hands pinned my arms. "Don't touch her, Byrne!" he warned me with such bitterness that I was forced to obey.

Smiling redly, licking her cannibal lips, the girl glided back to her ancient coffin; reposed herself within it. Slowly she pulled down the lid . . . and that was all.

As if in a dream, I allowed Clay to lead me back across the vast space to the spot whence we had come. And then the sunlight grew dim—and we were again in a pitch-dark passageway. I stumbled drunkenly into the study, where a dull lamp glowed. With blurred eyes I gazed out through the window—and saw the rain-drenched night.

I had come back to reality.

"Clay—my God!" I broke out. "That place—the sunlight—that woman from the tomb—"

Once more he was in his chair, his features more bony and bloodless than ever. He smiled. Then . . . you saw it,

She rose out of that ancient coffin, a creature of hell itself.

too? I'm not a madman? My blood's really being drained by that lovely vampire out of the Past?"

I nodded. "It's true!" I whispered. "It's true, God help us both! I . . . saw with my own eyes!" But I was too stunned, too stupefied, to say more; or to think clearly. I found my way to the guest-room that had been prepared for me; and I fell into a heavy, sodden slumber.

GREY dawn was streaking in through my window when a cautious tap at the door awakened me. I slipped into my dressing robe and opened the door. Marcia slipped into my room.

Her nightgown was clinging and sheer; her young-girl curves hinted themselves through the soft silk. She turned to me, her eyes wide and frightened. "Byrne—I didn't dare come until now. Clay hasn't slept until a few minutes ago. Tell me . . . did you l-learn anything. . . ?"

How could I say to her that I had watched her husband caressing an evil ghost-thing in woman's form? Without having her think me insane, how could I describe to her the scenes I had witnessed? And in truth, now that a new day was breaking, I was reluctant to believe that the past night's horrid events had actually transpired. I must have been deluded, I told myself. I had dreamed that tomb, and that superbly evil Princess of the Past. . . .

Closing the door, I summoned a smile for Marcia. "Give me a little more time, my dear," I soothed her. "I'll get to the bottom of Clay's trouble."

"Oh-h-h . . . if only you can . . . !" she moaned softly. And then she sagged weakly against me, with her arms clasped about my neck and sobs quivering her firm little breasts.

I held her and stroked her shoulders, trying to quiet her. But her nearness aroused all the old yearnings within me. The smooth texture of her skin sent leaping lances of longing through my veins. The faint fragrance of her golden hair was like wine, intoxicating me. Her lips were a tremulous temptation that I could not resist.

I kissed her. . . .

We clung together for a long, long while; and I thrilled to the sweet softness of her feminine body; grew giddy with the delirious happiness of embracing her. I could just glimpse the velvet-white area that separated her lovely breasts; my eyes returned again and again to the revealed upper slopes of those enticing rondures. . . .

But at last she slipped away from me; for she realized that her love belonged to Clay and not to me. I watched the rippling play of her hips and thighs under her nightgown as she went to the door and left me. And there was no more sleep for me, that dawn. I paced the room, thrumming and tense with a frustration that would be with me always. . . .

Clay slept the clock around, not rising until dusk that evening. Then he ate sparingly at dinner; motioned me up to his study. He closed the door, closeting us alone together. "Byrne—" he said harshly.

"Yes, Clay?"

The rain still pelting against his window made a whispering background of sound for his words. "Byrne, you don't consider me a madman, do you?"

I filled my pipe from his jar. "If you are—then I am, also."

His lips twisted; he rubbed his throat reminiscently, where white teeth had punctured his flesh and left tiny scars.

"Listen," he said. "Marcia's behind this!"

"Marcia—?" I gasped.

"Yes. I saw her today—when she thought I was asleep. She was mumbling incantations before some damned gruesome Isis-idol downstairs. Byrne—I think Marcia is the one that's enchanted me, bewitched me! She wants me to die. She wants to be rid of me!" He was almost hysterical.

I felt a sensation of dizzy nausea at the import of his accusations. "That's fantastic, Clay! It couldn't possibly be true!"

He grew more calm. "Very well. Perhaps I'm wrong. Will you do me a favor?"

"Yes."

His eyes glowed somberly. "Then go through that secret door—alone—by yourself—tonight. Now."

"You mean—you want me to—?"

"I want you to see if you can put an end to this accursed thing that's killing me, draining my blood! I'm helpless, Byrne. Helpless, I tell you! That dream-woman . . . she calls me. Always she calls me, summons me! I can't stay away from her when night falls. But maybe . . . if you go in my place . . . you can. . . " His voice trailed off, weakly.

I stumbled to my feet. "I'll go," I whispered dully.

HE LED me to the hidden panel; opened it. I went forth into darkness—and then brilliant sunlight.

It was the same as before; the rolling landscape, the far horizons, the blue sky and the brown hills. Surrounded by this fantastic enchantment, I trudged to that distant tomb. I spoke to the ancient sarcophagus; commanded it to open.

The lid raised. That dead-alive beauty from some hellish past glided toward me, smiling redly.

Chaos seethed in my brain. I wanted to kill her . . . and I wanted to take her in my arms, kiss her. . . . She laughed, evilly. "You cannot kill me, for I am deathless!" she whispered. "Only with a sharp stake of mistletoe through my heart can you destroy me. And you have not the courage to stab me . . . here." She unfastened her breastplates, so that her full white breasts were revealed under the thin draping of her gossamer robe.

And she was right. She had read my mind—and she knew that I could not wound such magnificent, alluring flesh. Sobbing at my own weakness, I caught her around the waist and pulled her against me.

Liquid flame seemed to sear me at the contact. As my lips welded against her mouth, the last of my self-control melted away. Her skin was snowy and warm, and smoother than the finest satin. Her whole body quivered as I carried her to that stone bench. . . .

LATER, she placed her mouth on my throat, and I seemed to feel the blood being drained from me. But I did not care. I was lost. The remembered, hellish ecstasy of her embrace still remained with me as she finished her gruesome feast; and I cried out to stay her as she glided back to her ancient coffin. I wanted more of her kisses; more of her demoniac love.

But the lid of the sarcophagus closed upon her; nor could I pry it open again. Weakly, I shambled back across the distance to the spot where enchantment began; and without realizing how it had come about, I found myself once more in Clay's study.

(Continued on page 95)

SMALL EVIL

[Continued from page 71]

barred cell window. I was nothing more: a prisoner; I was as helpless, as incapable of breaking the uncanny bonds that bound me as a prisoner is of crushing the steel bars between his fingers and leaping through.

And as night fell, I returned to the house.

I came there with trembling body, on silent creeping feet, with the awful hunger flaming high in me. I was panting, and the sweat was dripping from me; my lips thirsting for that scarlet flower of passion that carried death, I knew, in its embrace. I did not care.

Night lay thick in the deserted street, and silence in the old house. A door might have opened and swiftly closed as I made my way up the stairs; I would not have known. One thing, one thing alone burned vividly before me, and that was the golden vision of the woman.

Everything was the same: the drab room, the rumpled bed, the one dim light . . . and the statuette on the table. My eyes feasted on it. I knew its secret; to me, it—she— was alive. I knelt before it and stroked the smooth surface, and perhaps I talked to it. I do not know—I knew only that my fingers were tingling with the feel of it and that my head was heavy and whirling, my eyes protruding as they stared at that small evil beauty. As my eyes fell on my wounded wrist I laughed, laughed insanely.

THE room was darkening around me and I knew that she was coming again. Great shadows rose and fell and gathered together and built up into a towering mass of blackness. The soft eerie wailing was in my ears. A cold wind seemed to wash over me. Formless things seemed to move in the clammy darkness. This was another world, a world old as time, a nightmare world of nameless horror and evil—evil that sucked the life from me. And yet my whole soul hungered for it even while my brain reeled with dread.

Then she was there, more weirdly intoxicating, more alluring than before, more maddeningly beautiful. I had felt her sleek warm flesh against mine, I knew the promise of her red mouth. I groaned in abject surrender and stretched out my tense, trembling arms for her.

She seemed to yield for a moment. Then she was taut again and straining against me, and the scarlet bossom of her mouth was seeking mine and lingering over it, the moist warm lips fluttering. Unbearable ecstasy claimed me; she was locked to me as if our bodies were one.

I felt her fingers slipping down to my wrist, and through the swirling darkness I glimpsed the sheen of the sharp blade in her hand. . . .

I could not resist. All strength had flowed from me. I was a mute, unthinking thing, helpless before her, even though deeply within me somehow I knew that if the knife descended and the crimson stream burst out, the clean sunlight of the world of living men would never again shine in my eyes.

But I did not care. Nothing could have made me move or resist her save the incredible.

And the incredible happened!

As the blade hovered over the blue veins and the rich thirsty lips parted in anticipation, dimly I became aware of another shape—far off in the unreal darkness. A soft, slim form, vaguely white at first and then clearer as it moved rapidly forward; the shape of a girl. And my heart stopped and then beat violently within me as I saw that that pale face, beautiful even through the horror that showed on it, was the face of Joan!

THE golden woman bending over me became aware of her then and the full red lips drew back in a snarl. I struggled weakly to rise, but could not, my limbs were leaden; and in dumb terror I saw the spectral golden shape lash out at the girl, the razor-keen blade sweeping downward at her heart.

But miraculously it missed its mark! It ripped through Joan's clothing, and her soft round shoulder gleamed whitely through the rent. Before the knife could rise again she had flung her body against the other's and the knife fell away into the darkness. Like panthers the two were fighting with blind feline fury, ripping and clawing.

And as I stared, another shadowy crooked shape rose from the pool of darkness behind, and I saw

that it held the knife and was raising it high—

The sweat was pouring from me and I was moaning in agony. Then the blade was coming down—and with an effort that made my nerves coil within me I lurched drunkenly from where I lay and half fell against those two entangled bodies.

I heard an awful, shuddering scream, and I knew it was a scream of death. But that was all I knew.

THE REST is quickly told. It could not have been more than a half hour later that I came to consciousness. The room was flooded with light, and Joan's arms were around me, her tear-wet face pressed against mine, her half-clad body bent over me. I felt heavy and sluggish, my brain was misty and things would not stand still before my eyes—but I was sane. My eyes fell on the figure that sprawled on the floor, a knife-blade protruding grotesquely from the blood-splotched flesh.

It was Luciella! Luciella, her body covered with shining metallic gold paint, face almost unrecognizable under its exotic mask of cosmetics, a golden-bronze wig askew on her head.

Joan was sobbing, "The—the old man killed her. He struck at me just as you fell against us—and the knife missed me and—"

"But how—how did you—why are you here?" I stammered stupidly.

"The telegram!" she said. "The telegram you sent, saying you needed me—you needed me to save you. I got it today!"

"Telegram? I didn't—" Then

I said, "Where is the old man you say killed—her?"

"He ran from the room—ran when he saw that the knife had struck her."

We found him in the basement, a little later, when a semblance of strength had returned to me. And we found other things, too, back in that secret den: phials of a dark sluggish liquid that was human blood. It was for him that Luciella played her unholy masquerade; he gibbered out the whole grisly story to us. The mad idea of eternal life had grown in him as the years bent his body and sapped his strength. He used his daughter's beauty to lure men to the old house; besotted with drugs, helpless and inert in that dim room, adrift in a world of fantasy, they yielded to her spell, and she caught their blood in bowls while they lay unconscious and carried it to her father's greedy lips. . . .

But I remembered her lips over my wrist; the evil thirst must have grown in her too.

Keneidos died before they could get him to the chair. And the telegram—I must have sent it that day when the drug-spawned visions were crowding my brain.

I did not tell Joan that. I was content to crush her sweet young form to mine and find forgetfulness in her love.

DEALER IN DEATH

[Continued from page 63]

black laughter, shuddery and congealed. . . .

Laughter! Laughter from Lyala, the gypsy wench, who writhed and twisted upon the ground where she had been cruelly thrown. Lyala, not quite dead at the hangman's hands! Lyala, her smouldering eyes already glazing—and yet holding a flicker of inner glow—

Painfully came words from her broken, crushed throat. "Oh hangman—let the scales—fall from your eyes! You who killed—my mother—taste now—the bitter seeds—of madness—!"

He staggered to his feet and stumbled toward her, a frigid slime of fear seeping into his marrow. "You wench—!" he gasped. "What means this thing?"

"You . . . denounced my mother . . .and slew her . . . murdered her! But now . . . you pay . . the full price! Think ye . . . that I possessed . . . enough magic . . . to triumph over . . . the grave? Thou fool! I knew . . . no sorcery! The potion . . . I brewed . . . was without effect! I . . . tricked thee, oh hangman! Tricked thee . . . into hanging . . . the maid . . . of thy evil desires! She . . . died upon . . .thy gibbet! Ye killed her! *All that is left is her rotting corpse!*"

Then the nauseating truth dawned upon his reeling, tottering mind. He turned back to the body of the golden-haired Helen; *and he saw that her white flesh was already bloated and decomposing!* Putrescence had already set in;

and from the noxious orifice that had once been her kissable mouth, *a slimy white maggot squirmed!*

This, then, was the thing he had done! Lyala's gypsy potion, which draught he had swallowed an hour agone, had drugged his mind and dulled his senses so that he was receptive to the tawny girl's hypnotic power. Lyala had made him believe that Helen was alive; but now he knew the bitter, sickening truth. . . .

Madness burrowed into his brain. His reason cracked. He leaped with both feet upon the gypsy's supine form; his boot-heels sank murderously into her soft flesh. . . He jumped up and down on her quivering body until his feet had reduced her to a mass of bleeding flesh-pulp; until he was bathed in crimson beyond his knees. And as he killed, he shouted; he yelled fiendish imprecations into the night from the depths of his insane throat.

The night-watch came at a dead run, summoned by the hellish din. There were four of them. Their leader gasped: "By'r Lady—'tis the hangman! He's murdered a wench and dug up a corpse! Marry, He'll dance on his own gibbet!"

Which, in due course, happened.

ROOM OF DREAMS

[Continued from page 91]•

He was waiting for me, sunk deep in his leather chair. "You . . . saw her again, Byrne?"

"I saw her—may God have mercy on what's left of my soul!" I whispered. I felt drunk, sick. The study's walls seemed to shimmer and dance at a ridiculous distance.

"By hell!" he got to his feet. "You don't mean that you, too, have fallen under her spell?"

I nodded.

"We've got to do something, Byrne! We must!" Clay shouted, almost hysterically.

I realized the utter truth of what he said. Something must be done to break the weird fetters binding him—and myself—to that beautiful creature of evil. Otherwise, we would both continue to be drawn nightly through that damned enchanted door, into Egypt's past. We would both suffer ourselves to be drained of life-blood, until we were husks—empty corpse-shells, rotting and putrescent and forgotten.

Then something leaped into my mind.

"Clay!" I said. "A sharpened stake of mistletoe—driven through her heart —that will free us! It will kill her; send her back to hell where she belongs. She herself told me so; taunted me that I dared not destroy her. . . ."

My brother shuddered painfully. His lips twisted. "God! I couldn't do that, Byrne. I can't! I can't!"

"Then I shall," I said quietly. I was filled with a strange new courage that I could not comprehend. "Tomorrow night I'll break the spell, pierce the enchantment—and slay a fiend!"

THE remnants of a three-day rain still fell, that following morning. I clad myself in a slicker against the weather;

and with Marcia's sweet, troubled eyes asking me a question I dared not answer, I went forth in search of mistletoe.

All day I remained away from the house, roaming the woodlands and the distant hills. By early dusk, I had found what I needed. I sharpened the stake

Before that damned gruesome Isis-idol she mumbled her incantations.

to a murderous green point; concealed it beneath my coat as I headed back toward the mansion.

I approached it from the rear, through a copse of sodden trees; the path led by the old stables and servant-quarters toward the back of the property. These

quarters I knew to be no longer in use; so that I was a little surprised when I saw a light glimmering at the window of what had been the coachman's cottage in the old days when my grandfather was alive.

Curious about the light, I crept soundlessly to the window; peered inside. Then a vast, cold amazement gripped me.

My brother Clay was in there. He was not alone. A woman was with him; a dark, lissome, beautiful creature garbed in every-day raiment. *But she was the girl from the enchanted sarcophagus!*

She was with Clay on a battered sofa; in his arms. Through a broken pane in the window came her voice: "You're sure he doesn't suspect anything, darling? He doesn't realize that the tobacco you give him to smoke contains hasheesh?"

Clay laughed sardonically. "No; he doesn't suspect, baby. But the drug certainly works on him! He's swallowed the whole fairy-tale, hook line and sinker. Tonight he figures to kill you with a mistletoe stake. What a shock he'll get when he learns he's murdered Marcia!"

The woman's arms caressed him. "He'll hang, won't he? You'll inherit his share of the estate. And you'll be free of Marcia—free to marry me—"

I had heard enough to make my stomach retch. Clay—my own brother—had tricked me! He planned to make a murderer of me so that I would hang! He would have me murder Marcia, his wife; the girl I loved. He wanted my money—and his freedom.

For an instant I thought of springing through the casement, attacking him and his foul mistress. I saw the entire blinding truth. Clay planned to place Marcia in that sarcophagus, so that I would stab her. I would be under the influence of the hasheesh contained in the pipe-tobacco. . . .

Hasheesh! The drug of dreams; the drug that causes a man to see vast distances, where only short spaces exist.

The drug that leaves a man open to semi-hypnotic suggestion, so that he believes palpable impossibilities . . . That was what had duped me and fooled my senses . . . .

BUT I did not reveal myself to Clay and his woman. My thoughts turned with sharp suddenness to Marcia herself. I must go to her, warn her, tell her everything. Then I would take her away with me. Clay's plans were checkmated, now that I understood the truth. He would never make a murderer of me. He would never inherit my half of our family fortune. And meanwhile, Marcia and I would go to some distant land—toward happiness.

I ran to the mansion.

But Marcia was not there. I could not find her, though I searched everywhere. Then I knew that Clay must already have spirited her into the secret room; placed her in the sarcophagus to await death at my hands.

I raced to his study; sought frantically for the hidden spring that operated the concealed door. But my fingers encountered no lock, no mechanism. My efforts were fruitless. Bitter fury filled me; a fury that was impotent.

I tried to calm my jumping nerves. I must, I told myself, fight trickery with wile; combat craftiness with cunning. If I were to find Marcia, it must be through duping my brother Clay.

Slowly, I went to my guest-chamber. I drew forth my two matched briar pipes; filled one of them from my own pouch. I placed both back in my pocket.

And when I heard Clay coming into the house, I called to him; went with him to his study.

"Where's Marcia?" I asked him.

"She took a trip to town. I sent her —so that we'd be free to do what we

briars. The one I lighted was the one loaded with my own mixture.

Clay's eyes were on me, narrowly. He was waiting for the drug-smoke to have

She laughed evilly. "You cannot kill me, for I am deathless!"

must do, tonight," he answered slowly.

I studied him as he shoved his tobacco-jar toward me. I knew, now, what caused his cadaverous appearance. He had deliberately starved himself these past few months in order to worry Marcia; so that she would summon me from South America. His trick was obvious, now that I knew his motives.

I filled my empty pipe from his jar. Then, pretending to fumble in my pocket for a match, I succeeded in switching its effect on me. Remembering my symptoms of the past two nights, I pretended dizziness; mumbled thickly when I spoke. I showed him the sharpened stake of mistletoe. "To kill a she-demon!" I muttered.

His smile curdled my marrow. "You are ready, Byrne?"

"I'm . . . ready."

"Luck," he whispered; and he could not keep the triumph from his tone—although, had I been drugged, I would not have noticed it. He went to the secret panel, and it opened.

I went into the passageway—alone.

AGAIN I was in sunlight. But now, with my senses alert and my mind unfogged, I saw that it was only the harsh glare of overhead incandescents, cleverly concealed. The great vistas of landscape were, I perceived, nothing but painted scenery on the walls of this secret chamber within the house. And the fake tomb—a stage property—was just a few feet from me. Only under the influence of hasheesh would the distance seem the fourth part of a mile.

But I traversed the space slowly, dragging my feet; forcing myself to assume a sleepwalker's drugged movements. I gained the tomb; saw that the sarcophagus was open.

Marcia lay in that ancient coffin, relic of my grandfather's delvings in Egyptology. My beloved Marcia, swathed in the sheer robes which previously had been worn by the other woman. Marcia, with a black wig over her golden hair; with a veil upon her sweet features. Marcia, sleeping and anæsthetized by some drug . . .

Instead of plunging my stake through her heart, as Clay had wished, I lifted her in my arms. Her dainty, fragile form was etheral—and yet human, thrilling, utterly desirable and feminine. I turned; sped with her, back toward the door through which I had come.

And Clay stood before me, barring my way. His face was contorted with rage. "So—you know the truth!" he rasped.

He drew a knife.

I heard another sound behind me. It was the brunette girl. "Yes—kill him! Kill him, Clay! Kill both of them!" she shrilled. "They know too much—"

Clay threw his knife full at my chest.

I swerved, shielding Marcia with my body. The blade hurtled past me. I heard a wet, gurgling scream at my back. I pivoted.

Clay's mistress had taken the dagger's point in her heart. Its handle protruded sickeningly from the swelling mound of her left breast. She sagged to the floor; I think she was dead before she fell.

My brother mouthed a wild, insane oath. "Damn you to hell—you've made me kill her! You've made a murderer of me!" He leaped at me.

Marcia slumped from my arms; I met his savage attack. He was no match for me in his self-induced weakness. I smashed my fists into his jaw. "Trick me, eh?" I panted. "Make me think your blood was being sucked! Make me think my own veins polluted by that fake vampire! Make a killer of me!" I struck him again and again, until his bony face was a gory pulp of shapelessness. When he lay at my feet, I would have strangled him. But a voice halted me—

"Byrne—no! No, Byrne!"

It was Marcia, struggling to her unsteady feet. "My dearest!" I whispered as I went to her, took her trembling body in my arms.

Her sheer Egyptian robe was torn. Her lovely little breasts were almost wholly revealed; but she seemed not to care as she fused herself against me. "Byrne—I heard and saw—everything! He gave me a spinal injection before he brought me here; I was helpless, yet my mind was awake. Oh, Byrne, Byrne . . . to think I married a monster like that. . ."

"A monster who'll die on the gallows —for murdering his own mistress!" I said. "The trap he set for me was the one that closed on him instead. He is the killer, not I. And his mistress the victim, instead of you." I crushed her close to me, savoring the ripe warmth of her curves and lowering my mouth toward her parted lips.

"Byrne!" she whispered. "I . . . love you. . ."

I carried her out of that room of evil dreams. And when I had telephoned to the state police, I took her to my own chamber. There, in the darkness, she rested in my arms. . . .

THE VAULT

[Continued from page 83]

Then, because the light reached out ahead and showed him something else, he jerked to a halt. There at the foot of the cellar stairs stood the old woman, Aggie Bradley, leering at him; and the hag's withered claws gripped a sawed-off shotgun.

"So you thought you'd escape!" she sneered.

Andy stood rigid. Rosemary Hammond voiced a low cry of terror and shrank against him, shuddering. The old woman slowly advanced.

"Get back in the vault!"

They had no alternative. Yet as Andy drew the terrified girl back toward that grim threshold, he saw something else. At the top of the cellar stairs, something white, vaguely familiar, took form. The stairs creaked softly under descending feet.

The black walls of the death-vault seemed to close in with renewed hunger as Andy Scribner and the girl retreated into the room's dismal depths. The old woman leered at them from the doorway. Her beady eyes fastened on Andy, and her lips quivered with ugly laughter.

"Once you've found old Simeon's treasure," she hissed, "there's no escape. That's the way Simeon wanted it, and

that's the way it is. Money's a curse; you'd ought to have known that! And when old Simeon died, he vowed he'd have the last laugh by makin' other fools suffer the same as he did. Me, I'm helping him."

Rosemary Hammond shrank from the malevolence of the old woman's voice, flung her arms around Andy's rigid form and sobbed out her terror. At any other time, he might have thrilled to the nearness of her, might have felt his pulse quicken as her heaving bosom flattened against him and the sweet perfume of her hair stole into his senses. But now the voice of Aggie Bradley was like a dull saw scraping his brain. He could think of nothing else.

"I promise Simeon," the old woman muttered, "I'd carry on after he died. There'd be plenty of fools, I told him, seekin' after his treasure. But I'm gettin' old myself, so last week I begun to train someone else to keep up the work after I went. I guess you know what I'm talkin' about, all right, don't ye? And—" she leered at Rosemary—"maybe *you* do, too."

Andy Scribner licked his lips, said nothing. His arm tightened about the shuddering shape beside him, but he could not force himself to whisper words

The old woman slowly advanced. "Get back in the vault!"

of hope. Under the gaze of Aggie Bradley's glittering eyes, all the hope in his breast had fled.

"Last week," the hag sneered, "a pretty young girl come here seekin' after the treasure. She come at night, alone, so I had an easy time with her. I just showed her where the vault was, and closed the door on her. Then I done some thinkin'. *That* girl, I said to myself, would be the ideal person to carry on after I die.

"I left her in the vault for two days, and when I opened the door, she was out of her mind somewhat. The rest was easy. I just taught her a few of my own little tricks and threatened to lock her in the death-room again if she didn't obey me. She was willin' enough, all right. And clever, too, in spite of her twisted mind. *You* ought to know how clever she is, mister!"

ANDY was staring, not at the hag but at something beyond her. Something gorgeously beautiful, alluringly feminine, in a diaphanous gown which revealed lithe limbs, supple womanly curves, arching bosom. His blood had turned to ice. His breathing strangled him as the creature crept closer to Aggie Bradley's back.

Aggie heard the soft footsteps, turned, then grinned. "This here is my new helper," she cackled. "Ain't she lovely, though?"

Rosemary Hammond raised her head to stare.

It happened with almost unbelievable abruptness. One moment, Rosemary was clinging to Andy Scribner; next moment she had lurched sideways and was gaping in utter horror at the girl in the doorway. Her scream was a single blast that contained a name. *"Bertha!"*

That scream, filling the vault with its mad echoes, lured the old woman's attention away from Andy for a split second. Andy hurled himself forward.

The old woman's face twisted with sudden terror. She jerked backward, fumbled frantically with the weapon in her gnarled hands. A vast clap of thunder shook the vault's walls as the gun exploded, but Andy Scribner had reached his objective.

The rain of that shot ripped into his shoulder did not stop him. His hands closed convulsively, fingers and thumbs buried in the hag's wrinkled throat. Snarling horribly, he bore her to the floor.

She fought him like a wildcat, twisted her neck from his grasp and clawed at him with razor-sharp talons that drew blood from his cheeks. She screamed at him, cursed him, but the shotgun lay beneath her, out of reach, and Andy's clenched fists beat like sledges against her writhing face. At the last, he dragged her to her feet, hurled her across the room.

Spitting blood, she crashed against the far wall, swayed there for a moment, clawing at the air in front of her. Still conscious, she collapsed slowly, fell to her hands and knees. In the heat of the battle, her unkempt clothing had been ripped by Andy's clutching fingers. Her withered figure had a pathetic droop now as she attempted to crawl.

Andy turned away, took Rosemary Hammond in his arms. As he did so, a silent figure swayed past him and gazed down at the twisted shape on the floor.

Blood dripped from Andy's shoulder, but he hardly felt the agony of his wounds. Both he and Rosemary stared at the other girl, the alluring creature who not long ago had led Andy to the vault.

She had changed now. The downfall of the old hag seemed to have dazed her, left her mentally blank. When Rosemary whispered her name—"Bertha!"—she turned slowly, shook her head as if to clear it of some bewildering dream, and vacantly returned Rosemary's gaze. Then, like an automaton, she walked out of the vault.

"My sister," Rosemary said dully. "My—my sister."

And suddenly Andy Scribner realized what the twisted, crawling thing on the floor was trying to do! Eyes wide with horror, he stiffened. The old woman's withered hand, red with blood, was feebly reaching out to bear down on the sheet-iron slab in front of the treasure table.

With a hoarse cry Andy seized the girl beside him, hurled her over the threshold into the cellar, and staggered after her. Even as he lurched through the doorway, the iron bars were beginning their hideous descent. They clanged into place behind him. Trembling in every muscle, he took Rosemary in his arms again and turned.

Aggie Bradley's twisted body lay squarely across the oblong of iron. Her glazed eyes, wide open in death, stared back at him.

He reached out, gripped the iron ring

and turned it, but the grim bars remained in place. The weight of the woman's body on that fiendish counterbalance was sufficient to hold them there —forever.

Horror kept Andy Scribner silent. From the depths of the cellar behind him, the girl named Bertha came slowly forward, plucked at Rosemary's arm. "I—I want to go home," she whispered. "I'm so—so tired, Rosemary."

Andy turned. The agony in his shattered shoulder had crept to his vitals. His eyes flickered, breath sighed from his lips as he sank to the floor.

SUNLIGHT was streaming through the bedroom window when he regained consciousness. Rosemary, smiling tenderly, was beside him, her soft hands gently caressing his face.

"I sent my sister home," she said quietly. "She—she's all right now. She remembers nothing of what happened here." Then, after a moment of hesitation: "I—I lied to you when I said I was looking for Simeon's money. I wasn't, really. I—you see, I knew my sister had come here seeking the treasure, and I was sure something horrible had

happened to her. So I came here, alone, and—found a part of the cellar where the earth was freshly turned."

Andy stared at her. "When you were digging in the cellar you found something. You must have. I heard you scream."

"I—I found what was left of some of the other people who came here," she confessed.

Andy drew her closer. Somehow, her nearness seemed to drive evil memories from his mind and ease the aching throb in his shoulder. The pressure of her slim young body against his was soothing and wonderful.

He drew her half-parted lips down to his own, sighed contentedly as soft curves snuggled warmly, like purring kittens, against his chest. This was a new kind of dream, thrilling and full of promise. With her lips still clinging to his, and low murmuring sounds in her throat, he closed his eyes.

Later, perhaps, he would find a hacksaw, cut his way through those gruesome iron bars in the cellar, and discover if old Simeon really had hidden a fortune in that black room of horror. But for now he had treasure enough.

POCKET OF BLACKNESS

[Continued from page 17]

Then he turned his attention back to the girl on the table. He put the blade of the knife against her shrinking flesh.

The man's saturnine mouth crooked in an evil grin. His hands began to quiver and his breath whistled through his thin nostrils. He wouldn't be thinking of Pinky now, or anyone except Tess, who

lay with eyes closed, still as marble save for the spasmodic shudder that swept every few seconds along her slender limbs.

Pinky got the edge of the point of masonry against the ropes. He moved his wrists back and forth with a sawing motion. He felt the stone rasp through skin and flesh, and could have screamed with the agony of it. But he bit his tongue till blood filled his mouth, and was silent.

The man in the chair groaned: "Damn you, Griffin—damn you, damn you!" He fought vainly against the ropes that held him. His gray eyes flickered toward Pinky, saw his motions and brightened momentarily. His expression encouraged Pinky frantically.

"Ha!" chuckled the one with the knife. "Don't miss any of this, Thane. I want you to remember it all your life. Maybe it will teach you not to poke your nose into other folks' affairs!"

Pinky couldn't saw his wrists any longer. It was too painful. Hunger and cold and fear had weakened him a a point where he was sure he would faint in another minute. He wanted to faint, wanted to close his eyes and lean back and let fate take its evil course.

Then Sara stirred beside him. He saw her eyes blaze with anger as she looked toward the girl on the table. She looked at Pinky appealingly. She expected *him* to do something!

New strength seemed to flow into Pinky's jaded body. His stringy muscles bulged. Abruptly the ropes holding his wrists parted and he felt the sting of circulation clear to his fingertips.

There wasn't a second to waste, if the girl on the table was to be saved from the gloating fiend. Pinky couldn't take time to cope with the knots at his ankles. But if he could push himself erect and hop forward, he could throw himself upon the masked man, whose back was toward him.

He struggled upward. He leaned forward and hurled himself, his hands outstretched. As he sprang a sharp cry burst from the lips of Tess. . . .

THE man, intent on the white form before him, had placed his knife on the table. Pinky's left hand closed over the blade and tightened, not minding that the steel bit into his palm. His right hand caught the neck of the bottle on the table and knocked the candle from it, plunging the crypt-like chamber into utter blackness.

A screeched oath rang in his ears and clawlike fingers found his neck and moved around to the soft part of his throat. Desperately Pinky swung the bottle. It struck a skull and shattered. The fingers left his throat and there was the sound of someone reeling backward, cursing madly.

A gun blasted, its flash lighting the chamber brilliantly for a split second. Pinky saw the evil Griffin crouched, aiming for another shot at him. There was an awful pain in his right shoulder where the first bullet had struck.

He groped toward the man in the chair blindly, battling faintness. Again and again the gun crashed and flared and once Pinky felt hot metal scrape his ribs. But he reached the young man, fumbled for his wrists and pressed the blade of the knife against the ropes. Then he fainted. . . .

The icy needles of rain in his face brought him to. Pinky lay with his head in a woman's lap—in Sara's lap—just in front of the ancient church. Sara sat quite still, her hand gently stroking his hair, but there were a lot of people milling around them. Some of the people wore uniforms and badges.

Pinky thought: *The cops! Now I'll get the chair!*

Someone was talking. Pinky recognized the voice of Thane, the young man who had been tied in the chair. He looked up and, in the light of policemen's flashlights, saw him sitting on the steps of the church with Tess cradled in his arms. He had taken off his coat and wrapped it around her, but the coat wasn't buttoned and Pinky could see flashes of gleaming white skin quite plainly. It made him think of Sara, lost to him now that he was a prisoner.

But what was it the young man was saying?

"That's me, lieutenant—Gordon Thane, of the Secret Service. Tess and I have been on the trail of those counterfeiters for two months.

"We suspected Maynard Howell, and Tess, my fiancee, got a room in the hotel where he lived and kept her eye on him. We couldn't find anything in his room, so tonight we decided to follow him when he went out. He was too quick for us, though. He beat it, all dressed up in evening clothes and a silk hat, out of one side of the lobby while we were watching the other side.

"The house dick tipped me off, but it would have been too late if Howell hadn't unexpectedly stepped into a holdup. I just happened to see the holdup man run away after slugging him." Thane's eyes were fastened on Pinky, moving over him as though to make sure what he looked like. Pinky thought

of his description as it was written in the police files. Five feet seven, one hundred and forty pounds, pale complexion, blue eyes, brown hair.

Thane said: "The holdup man was a big guy. Weighed two hundred pounds, at least, I should say. He was swarthy and wore flashy clothes."

Pinky took a deep breath. So this government cop wasn't going to give him away, after all! He looked up into Sara's face and managed a smile.

"And you found Howell knocked out, eh?" one of the cops said.

Thane nodded. "When he came to, he said he wasn't hurt bad and he wouldn't let the police take him to a hospital. Said he had an important date. So Tess and I were able to follow him, after all.

"We followed him to this building beside the cemetery. He walked up to an engraving plant run by this bird Griffin on the eighth floor. It was in that plant the two of them turned out their phony five-dollar bills, in a secret room next to the regular engraving plant.

"I heard them quarrel through the door. Howell had the idea that Griffin had tried to have him killed —that the holdup was really an attempt at murder. They had a fight and Griffin smacked Howell over the head with a hammer. Then he dragged Howell into the regular engraving shop and switched on the lights for a minute and threw Howell out the window. He struck a gravestone and broke his back."

"That blue light!" Pinky gasped.

Thane grinned at him. "A mercury vapor lamp. I'll bet it seemed bright down here in the darkness."

He continued: "I didn't't break in then, because I had an idea Griffin would have the plates hidden somewhere else. I followed him when he left, and I was right. He had them hidden in the basement of the old church, in a room nobody ever used, where he could sneak in and get them easily at night. But Griffin was smarter than I gave him credit for. He suspected that he was being followed, and he waited for me in the church and got the drop on me. He tied up both Tess and me.

"He'd already spotted my assistants, here, and captured them—"

The lieutenant snorted: "Your assistants? This jailbird and this dame—?"

"Sure," Thane lied. "I thought I might need help, so I asked 'em to stay close. As it happened, Griffin wouldn't ever have been caught if Tess and I had been alone. My assistant managed to get loose and free me, and helped me tackle Griffin. I killed him with his own gun."

"And there's a reward!" the lieutenant said.

"Five thousand dollars. Tess and I are willing to split it even."

Pinky's mind couldn't take in any more. Four hundred and eighty dollars Sara had in her bosom— and not in counterfeit five-dollar bills, either—and twenty-five hundred dollars was due them in rewards. He wasn't a murderer slated for the chair; he was, on the contrary, a hero to whom the law owed a debt of gratitude. And he had Sara—

"I gotta go," he murmured. "I don't like this spot! I'm sleepy!"

"We called an ambulance to take you to the hospital," the cop informed him. "You're shot twice. Not bad, though—"

"Nix," protested Pinky. He winked at Thane, who was cuddling Tess close. "My boss, the G-man, can tell you why I don't want to go to no hospital. He knows what it's like to be crazy about a dame. I want to be where my girl can nurse me.

"You tell the ambulance guy to take me and Sara to the best hotel in the burg. You can send a doctor up to our room, but he can't stay long. Me and Sara have got a lot of things to talk about. We gotta decide on a preacher to marry us and where we're gonna live and what we're gonna do with our money, and all that stuff."

SIX WERE SLAIN

[Continued from page 37]

was tired. The knife fell from my hand and I staggered to my bed. What happened after that I do not know. My weariness was like a devouring drug, and I could not even reply to my companions' questions. I slept.

That, señorita, is the truth. *I did not kill Jose and The Young One.* Even in my sleep I did not kill them, for had I done so there surely would have been blood upon my

hands, or upon my clothing, when I awoke.

Yet when my eyes at last opened, *señorita*, Jose and The Young One did not answer my call. The battered tin clock on the table told me it was late afternoon, but the silence all about me was like that of midnight. I sat on the edge of my bed and shook my head to clear the mist from my brain, and realized that I was alone.

I staggered to my feet and shouted again and again for my comrades, but there was no answer. Even then I kept on shouting, because the mocking echoes of my own hoarse voice were better than the silence.

I found The Young One in the corridor. His face wore a puzzling smile, and he lay on his back with his knees bent toward the ceiling. His eyes were open, *señorita*. His lips looked as though they were expecting a kiss.

He had been stabbed through the heart, but there was no knife near him.

Jose I found at the foot of the steps. His body lay sprawled on the stone floor and his head lay in a soft pillow formed by his mop of hair. He, too, was smiling. He, too, had been stabbed. But I found no knife.

That, *señorita*, is how they died. As God is my witness, I am telling the truth!

FOR three weeks I lived alone in the fortress. Three horrible weeks! I talked to myself constantly, and when I talked the grim walls threw my voice back at me in an effort to drive me mad. I buried

Jose and The Young One, and visited their graves every day. At night I barricaded myself in the sleeping room, for fear that I, too, would be overtaken by the same ghastly fate which had seized my comrades.

Not once did I venture far from the entrance to the fortress, above ground. Fear kept me from visiting the courtyard again, or exploring the ruins. Fear haunted me day and night and gave me no rest. A man can go mad with such terrors and such loneliness, *señorita*. They say I *am* mad. Perhaps I would have been in another few days. But the soldiers came first.

They questioned me and I told them what had happened. They stared at me queerly. I was sane, and I knew it, but they believed otherwise. When I told them of the marble statue they demanded to see it, and I said to them: "No! In the name of God, no!" But they forced me to lead them into the buried vaults of that temple of horror.

It took me more than an hour, *señorita*, to open the entrance, even though I had twice seen the marble woman do it. There were six of us when we descended into the depths. Every step of the way I begged them to turn back, but they were armed with torches and weapons, and I suspect they were more interested in the golden images of which I had told them, than in the marble woman. The soldiers of Greco Zamidas are ever eager for loot!

They were like madmen, *señorita*, when they discovered the riches of the temple. They seized all they could carry. Then I thought they would be satisfied, but no, they

must explore every room, every corridor of that weirdly wonderful world of treasure.

And so, when I had all but given up hope of finding the marble woman, we came upon her. It was in a room that fairly glittered with golden wealth, and there was an altar, and she stood there awaiting us.

The soldiers looked at her, and looked at me, and laughed. "This thing came to life?" they jeered. "Why, the fool is insane! He is lying to save his precious neck!" Two of them strode up to her and put their hands on her, slapping her marble body, her lovely curves in crude jest.

There was one soldier, *señorita,* who did not laugh. He paced forward very slowly and examined the woman from a distance of two or three feet, and he studied for a long while the inscriptions on the golden altar.

"This," he said, "is a virgin of the Sun. I have seen similar statues in other Aztec ruins. According to the historians, a beautiful maiden was worshiped each year, for a full year, and then sacrificed. She was sacred. Death was the penalty for touching her."

That is what he said, *señorita,* and he crossed himself. But the others merely laughed.

YOU have heard, perhaps, of the wealth that Greco Zamidas' soldiers brought back from that ruined city. You have heard also, no doubt, how two of the soldiers were slain during the long march through the jungle. They were murdered in their sleep. I, Pancho,

You think you *can't* learn Music?
Just try this! →

Easy as A-B-C
Look at the notes above — they are: F-A-C-E. Could anything be simpler to remember? You have already begun to learn to read music. And it's just as easy to *play*, for a remarkable invention, the "Note-Finder," tells you just where each note is located on the piano.

Look at Pictures and Play
Just imagine! Instead of spending tedious hours in study, instead of puzzling over obscure points, you look at clean-cut pictures that make every step as clear as day. Even children not yet in their teens soon learn to play by this fascinating print-and-picture method.

Which instrument do you want to play?
Here's *Free Proof* you can learn quickly — at home

IF YOU have ever had any desire to play a musical instrument—if you have ever longed for the good times, the popularity and friendships that music makes possible, then here is amazing proof that you CAN learn to play — easily, quickly, in spare time at home. What's more, in just a short time from today, you can actually be PLAYING. Yes, playing the piano, the violin, or whichever instrument you please. Playing the latest popular songs, the old-time favorites, even classical music.

No Knowledge of Music Required

Forget all you have ever heard about music being hard to learn. Dismiss your fears of tedious study and practice. Never mind if you do not know a single note of music.

This modern way to learn music will open your eyes! It's *easier* than you ever thought possible—and it's FUN. No old-fashioned drudgery, no tiresome drills and exercises. Instead, you start learning to play real tunes by note almost at once. You are thrilled to discover that you can actually create music! Soon you are experiencing the joys of musical self-expression. Soon you are winning popularity; you are being showered with compliments and applause.

Make Money, too!

Perhaps you have never thought of making money with music. But you may be pleasantly surprised to find how many opportunities it brings! Others have quickly started turning spare hours into cash and not a few have been launched on brilliant musical careers.

Does it all seem "too good to be true?" Then send for the Free Proof. Mail the coupon for the fascinating illustrated booklet that tells all about this wonderful way to learn music at home—in just a few minutes a day—without a private teacher, without any special talent or previous training. With the booklet you'll also receive a free Demonstration Lesson that shows exactly how it is done.

FREE—Just Mail Coupon

Over 700,000 others have already been convinced. Surely, if *you* earnestly want to learn to play, you owe it to yourself to examine the proof. There is no cost or obligation in writing. Just mention the instrument that interests you. If you do not already own one, we can arrange to supply it on easy terms. U. S. School of Music, 1862 Brunswick Building, New York, N. Y.

SEND FOR FREE DEMONSTRATION LESSON

PICK YOUR FAVORITE

Piano	Mandolin	Organ
Violin	Ukulele	Drums and
Guitar	Cornet	Traps
Accordion	Trumpet	Harmony
Saxophone	Harp	and
Cello	Clarinet	Composition
Hawaiian	Trombone	Voice and
Guitar	Flute	Speech
Banjo	Piccolo	Culture

U. S. School of Music,
1862 Brunswick Bldg.,
New York, N. Y.

Gentlemen: Please send me Free Proof that I can learn to play the .... including your illustrated booklet and Demonstration Lesson.
Have You
Instr. ?.............

Name.....................................

Address..................................

City....................... State..............

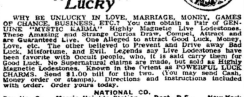
am accused of slaying them. They were the two who touched the marble statue, *señorita*. And it was not I who killed them.

So you see, I am to die for crimes I have not committed, *señorita*. Six men they say I have murdered. Two of them I did destroy, but it was not murder. The other four I did not lay a hand on.

The firing squad? I do not fear it. I shall never face it. You see, *señorita, I too touched the marble statue! And I knew you the moment you stepped into my prison cell. Do you think I could forget, after that glorious night in the temple?*

They told me, *señorita*, that I would be visited by a beautiful woman who had searched the face of every prisoner who was brought here. When they told me that, I knew you would find me. Ah, you are smiling! You read my thoughts! Is it too much to ask, my beloved, that you read also my desires? That you kiss me again the way you kissed me that other night?

Death will be but a small price to pay, my darling, if first you will let me hold you in my arms again, with your lips burning mine and your warm white body quivering to my caresses. If only I may see you once more as you were in the temple . . . Ah, my beloved, that is better! How beautiful you are! How my heart burns when you are so close to me!

Your lips, *señorita*. Your cool white bosom against my chest. Your glorious body trembling in my embrace. What fools they were, my adored one, when they laughed at me and called me mad! Any one of them would sell his soul for this moment that is mine . . . even though the knife . . . is already . . . quivering . . . in your . . . hand!

Bright Isle of Enchantment

[Continued from page 25]

"Rehearsals don't begin till Friday?" Campion asked.

"No."

"Any dates or anything before then?"

"Nothing important."

"My car's close by. Let's get in and spend five days in French Canada. Have you been there? There are quaint little towns where you go into the inns and sit with your glass of beer or *vin rouge* and chat with the natives. It's quite like France. What's the matter?"

"I've got to go home to get a few clothes. Haven't you?"

"I didn't think about it," said Campion, realizing that he had been about to start for Canada in evening clothes.

THEY left an hour later, and by morning were far away, speeding northward. They conversed but briefly, in snatches only, because both were overcome by the same feeling for each other. Her presence in the car beside him was maddening to Campion, because he had to drive and drive until some time that afternoon. The scent of her, the allurement of her made his senses ache.

And all the while there was the consciousness of Nora Clinton, the

only woman he had ever loved with his soul, lying dead deep down beneath the waters of the Atlantic, and that drive beside Kay Wynne was the most unhappy afternoon he had ever spent in his life.

They reached a hotel in Vermont late that afternoon, and Campion was alone with Kay at last. The evening before, a stranger, now a woman passing as his wife. Probably just an episode to her. Men don't ask those questions. But he recalled how his hands trembled as he bent over her and held her face close to his, and the little sigh with which she came into his embrace. . .

"CHARLEY, don't look back! Don't look back!"

That seemed to be Molly's voice, coming from an infinite distance. But Campion hardly heeded it.

Kay's murmuring laugh in the circle of his arms, and, afterward, the masses of black hair that fell over him as her head rested upon his shoulder.

"Where are you?" whispered Campion in awe. "Oh God, where are you?"

"Sleeping on my roof-top in Florida, Charley," answered Kay Wynne. "Old Harry's away, and I'm waiting for the boy-friend. But I'm sentimentalizing over you while waiting for him. That's why you see me."

"Then I'm dead," whispered Campion. "I love you, Kay!"—but he didn't mean it.

He turned in pursuit of her as she ran, laughing, away—and suddenly he found himself alone. There was no longer either Kay or Nora Clinton. Only the meadows

of asphodel, and dim figures in the distance.

Suddenly the memory of Kay vanished, as the memories of those other women had done. There remained only the thought of Nora. And Nora was gone!

Frantically Campion began running to and fro, searching for her, calling her. No answer came.

BUT Lady Molly was at Campion's side, and, at the sight of her dripping clothes, the idea that had haunted him, that he was dead, disappeared. They must have found some land, they had been delirious, hallucinated. . . .

"Where is he?" cried Molly, seizing Campion by the arm. "That old man? Oh God, Charley, I saw Hubert."

"I saw him too."

"Then I saw a man I've never told you about, Charley. A boy I loved more than my own soul, long before I met Hubert. I wasn't built to be a one-man woman, Charley, but after that first love of mine no other man—there never was any other man. Hubert knew about him. . . .

"You see, I was only a girl of eighteen, at school in Switzerland. And this boy was a young Englishman staying at the hotel near by. We fell in love the minute we saw each other. I used to steal out of the dormitory at night and meet him on the mountainside . . .

"He married a show-girl before I had left the boarding-school. I never believed in men again, until I met Hubert. That was a different love. That was something of the soul. Charley, everybody knows about your affairs in New York, but I have always thought there was never anybody but Nora Clinton for you."

"Never anybody else," said Campion.

"I saw Hubert, and he—he's gone," she sobbed. "That old man told me not to look back. What did he mean? I thought he meant not to turn my head, but perhaps he meant looking back—on the past—"

The old man was beside them. There was a look of pitying sadness on his face, but there was also something so divine there that the two clung to him like children.

"I know we've lost them," cried Campion. "But if we're dead, can't we meet our beloved ones again?"

"You are not dead."

"Kill us, then!"

The old man shook his head. "What you saw were images. Never, never once has a man gone down into the gates of death and brought a loved one back. Life and death are hard—but there are compensations on the other side. And there's a very merciful Judge, up above."

"Who are you?" Campion cried.

"Only a guide. Your time had not come, but you were so close to it that a little door was opened, so that you would understand."

Campion looked desperately about him, but there was no sign of any human figure now, except that of Lady Molly.

AND suddenly the asphodel meadows were shaken by a terrific storm. The wind howled about them, the rain pelted them. Cam-

pion caught Lady Molly in his arms and held her against the storm's fury.

There was no longer earth beneath them, only, the raging fury of the sea. But they were clinging to something, and, in a streak of lightning that clove the tropic night, Campion saw that it was the airplane.

Then he understood what had happened. Molly and he had been stunned by the swift immersion of the craft in the ocean; all that had happened since had been illusion. Some fighting instinct had enabled them to hold on.

But there *was* land close beside them. A coral reef, against which the waves were thundering, and smooth water beyond, and, beyond that, palm trees bending beneath the wind, and a tangle of tropical undergrowth.

Campion clung to the half-submerged plane. "She's going in through the entrance to the lagoon!" he cried. "We'll be safe in a few minutes."

But those were perilous minutes, when each moment a wave seemed on the point of dashing them against the jagged teeth of the coral. And then somehow—miraculously they were through, and the current was bearing them toward the island, over a calm lagoon.

Exhausted, Campion dragged the sea-soaked plane up onto the sand. The storm was dying down now, dawn was in the sky. Hand in hand, Campion and Molly struggled up the slope, and dropped beneath the palm trees.

Like two children they lay there,

holding each other, while the dawn brightened, and the lashing of the surf lessened, and the warm Polynesian day brightened in the east.

IT WAS light enough to see the plane now, as she lay on the sands. "Well, we've got food and water," said Campion. "And we can hold out here for quite a time. They're sure to pick us up. Too bad we had to come down, but I'm glad you're safe."

He patted her hand affectionately.

"You'd best get out of those wet things and hang them in the sun," he said.

"And you too," laughed Molly.

They moved apart instinctively. They were too good friends to have any squeamishness, but they had always retained their traditions, even in the close association of a plane. Campion stripped and hung his clothes on a scrubby palm, and sat down by the water, thinking.

Of course all the events of the night before had been hallucination, and yet they had left an indelible impression upon his mind.

He saw how, if there is any spiritual mating, the women with whom he had solaced himself after Nora's death, had come as a barrier between them.

"I'm going to get me a wife when I get back to New York, and be faithful to her for the rest of my days," he said to himself. "I shall never tell her about Nora. That's something of the past. If there is the merciful Judge up above the old man spoke about, maybe after death—maybe—"

He sighed, got up, and found that his clothes were dry. He put on shirt and trousers, and strolled bare-footed to where Molly and he had been sitting together.

"Hello, Molly," he called. "All tight and dry. How are you feeling, lady?"

"Oh, Charley, it takes a woman's clothes so much longer to dry than a man's," came a voice from behind a shrub.

"Well, if you're respectable, come out and let me see you."

MOLLY came out from behind the shrub. She was bare to the thighs, and wore a pair of step-ins, and, over them, a flying-shirt, a short, waist-long garment, cut low in the neck and leaving the arms exposed. She came forward, pulling it over her breasts and buttoning it up. There was something charming in her frankness, her disregard of herself as a woman.

"I'm going down to salvage our stuff soon," said Campion. "Molly, were we both dreaming the same dream last night?"

"Charley, do you mean to say— Oh, was it true? Were we in some half-living and half-dead condition where we could—could see the dead?"

Campion put his arm about her, but didn't answer her. She knew his answer from the way he held her. And there was something infinitely comforting in her warm presence. He hadn't thought of Lady Molly much except as a good sport; now he was seeing her as a woman, almost for the first time.

He looked at the long, tanned legs crossed beneath the little step-

Real Life and *Romance!*

You will be amazed and thrilled by the exploits of fiction's Ace Investigators in tales filled to the brim with danger and mystery set on a background as truly modern and *real* as its heroes are red-blooded and its heroines are alluringly beautiful.

PRIVATE
DETECTIVE
STORIES

On Sale At All Newsstands Dec. 27

ins, at the soft bosom tenting the shirt, and thought how very lovely she was.

Very lovely, because each of them had had his dead, and each of them had memories of other loves, and Campion wanted only a wife who would help him to forget, and to go on with the difficult business of being a man.

The warmth of her seemed to permeate him. A great new tenderness was growing in him. He would never love her as he had loved Nora Clinton, and she would never love him as she had loved the two men in her life, but they were companionable, they were comrades. . . .

"I was thinking," said Campion, after a long silence, "I've been pretty much of a damned fool, playing around with showgirls. If we ever get out of this, I want to settle down with a woman who understands that life is either a tragic or a comic thing, according to the way you look at it. I want a woman of my own, always, and I'm not going to play around again. Will you marry me, darling?"

LADY Molly looked at Campion. "I've been more in love with you than with any man I've ever known," she said. "Yes, of course I will. You know, dear, we're both mature people. I think we both have rather high-strung natures, and we've been taking it out by flying and adventure. I think married life would be a much simpler way out for both of us."

In the glory of her kiss, Campion felt a sudden and complete reconciliation with life. Life was made that way. If there was survival, he would meet Nora Clinton again. And he remembered the words, "In heaven there is neither marrying nor giving in marriage, for they are as the angels." Campion knew that he had found reality.

BODY DIVIDED

[Continued from page 49]

floor—one dead, the other spilling his blood in an ever widening crimson pool.

Don let the knife slide from his hand, went up to Purvis, and took the revolver from him. He forced

When answering advertisements please mention Spicy Mystery Stories him down into the chair. Purvis sat there, trembling. Don turned and beckoned to the nurse.

"No, no!" she screamed. "Damn you, damn you, damn you! Look what's he taken!"

Shrieking hysterically, she opened the door and darted away. Don turned to Purvis, who was replacing in a drawer a bottle containing some white tablets.

There was a smile on the little doctor's face now and his voice was calm in spite of the uncontrollable twitching of his mucles. "Yes, I shall be a dead man in half an hour, and there's no remedy," he said. "I've got a written confession here, Lancaster. I foresaw all this. But Emerson picked me up out of the gutter, and he knew . . . enough to send me to the penitentiary for fifty years. I had to do what he told me. But I prepared this confession, because I knew it couldn't go on. Check it over with me, Lancaster, and witness my signature."

"SO Emerson was not her uncle?" Don asked as he put aside the typewritten sheets.

"Her half-brother by a former marriage of old Emerson's. The will cut him off with fifty cents. When Mary was younger she was a nervous, hyper-tense, sensitive child. Cyrus Emerson forced me and another doctor to pronounce her insane. He had been known as her uncle, and, in that guise, he obtained a court order authorizing him to be her guardian."

"She isn't mad?"

"She never was mad! But I found her easily suggestible, and I persuaded the unconscious part of her mind, through hypnotism, that there were two different personalities in her, which accounted for the slight difference in the shade of her eyes. I could make her assume either the 'Mary' or the 'Betty' role by mere suggestion. That electrical apparatus is a fake, devised merely to delude her.

"I kept her under drugs for a long time. We wanted to drive her into actual insanity, so that Emerson could remain in charge of the property. Then you came! She got away one night and went to you. We saw you watching the house, and Emerson insisted you were a detective, and that you must be killed. He forced me to hypnotize Mary to make her kill you, so that

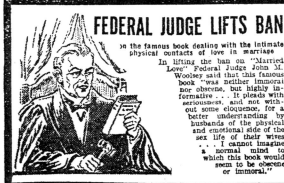

she could be confined for life as a homicidal maniac.

"But I made one mistake! I had heard that, even under hypnotism, no patient will commit an act that is contrary to his moral convictions. I knew a patient would stab with a paper knife at command, but I had heard he would refuse to commit actual murder with a butcher-knife.

"I didn't believe it, but it's true! I've learned something more, Lancaster."

Purvis's speech was growing thick. There was a quizzical smile upon his lips.

"No pain," he mumbled. "I'll feel no pain."

"You were a fool to kill yourself," said Don. "Isn't there an antidote? I might have—well, you are less guilty that Emerson."

"Don't—want—to live. Too—tedious, Lancaster."

SHRIEKS came to Don's ears, the voices and footsteps of men. They were coming along the passage. They burst into the room, half a dozen of the townsmen, holding Miss Masson, a raving, screaming madwoman, her clothing drenched with blood from a self-inflicted wound.

At sight of the two dead men, the half-nude girl on the floor, and Don, they recoiled, uttering shouts of horror. But two of them still held Miss Masson, who was fighting madly. Blood was still spouting from a wound in her throat.

Her struggles grew weaker. Suddenly she slumped in her captors' arms. Through the horrific silence came Purvis's last words:

"My—confession. Miss Emerson

—never mad. Plot—trick—conspiracy. Emerson and Pugh—quarreled over the girl and—killed each other. I've taken poison because—because—"

Which was not bad for Purvis, Don thought afterward. A kind of last-minute atonement for the errors of his shoddy life. His eyes rolled upward, he smiled once more at Don, and suddenly slumped forward in his chair.

With that Don ceased to be aware of anybody in the room except Mary Emerson. He went over and gathered her into his arms. He looked about, saw a rug upon the lounge. He carried her toward it, wrapped the rug about her. Cradling her in his arms, he made his way out of that house of horror.

"I'm taking her to my cabin," he said, when somebody intercepted him. "Send a woman to take care of her till the police come. That'll be all."

They helped him put her into a car and drove to the edge of the trail. There Don picked Mary up in his arms again and carried her to his cabin.

He placed her on the cot, and covered her lovely form with the blanket, as he had done that first night he met her. Soon the woman from the village would come, and, later, the State police. There was much to go through, but Purvis's confession would straighten it all out.

The Forbidden Secrets of Sex are Daringly Revealed!

AWAY with false modesty! At last a famous doctor has told *all* the secrets of sex in frank, daring language. No prudish beating about the bush, no veiled hints, but TRUTH, blazing through 576 pages of straightforward facts.

Love is the most *magnificent ecstasy* in the world... know how to hold your loved one, don't glean half-truths from unreliable sources. Now you can know how to end ignorance... fear... and self denial!

Everything pertaining to sex is discussed in daring language. All the things you have wanted to know about your sex life, information about which other books only vaguely hint, is yours at last.

MORE THAN 100 VIVID PICTURES

The 106 illustrations leave *little* to the imagination... know how to overcome physical mismating... know what to do on your wedding night to avoid the torturing results of ignorance.

Some will be offended by the amazing frankness of this book and its vivid illustrations, but the world has no longer any use for prudery and false modesty.

Don't be a *slave* to ignorance and fear. Enjoy the rapturous delights of the perfect *love life!*

Lost love... scandal... divorce... can often be prevented by knowledge. Only the ignorant pay the *awful penalties* of wrong sex practises. Read the facts, clearly, startlingly told... study these illustrations and grope in darkness no longer.

SEND NO MONEY!

To show you our faith in your satisfaction with this amazing book, we are offering it to you on trial. You send no money—just fill out the coupon below and then when it arrives, in plain wrapper, pay the postman $2.98 plus postage. Keep the book five days, then if you are not completely satisfied, send it back and we will refund your money immediately without question. "Eugenics and Sex Harmony" will not be sold to minors.

576 DARING PAGES

ATTRACT THE OPPOSITE SEX!

Know *how to enjoy* the thrilling experiences that are your birthright... know how to attract the opposite sex... how to hold love.

Are you an awkward novice in the art of love-making? Or, a master of its difficult technique? Knowledge is the basis of the perfect, satisfying love life. Ignorance leads to fear, worry, disease and shame. End ignorance *today*. You owe it to yourself—to the one you love—to read this book NOW!

PREVENT DISEASE — STOP WORRYING — BANISH FEAR — OVERCOME SHAME

KNOW THE AMAZING TRUTH ABOUT SEX and LOVE

EUGENICS AND SEX HARMONY

FORMERLY $5 NOW ONLY $2.98

State Age When Ordering

Over 100 Graphic Illustrations

WHAT EVERY MAN SHOULD KNOW

The Sexual Embrace
Secrets of the Honeymoon
Mistakes of Early Marriage
Venereal Diseases

Can Virility Be Regained
Sexual Starvation
Glands and Sex Instinct
The Truth About Abuse

WHAT EVERY WOMAN SHOULD KNOW

Joys of Perfect Mating
What to Allow a Lover to Do
Intimate Feminine Hygiene
Birth Control

How to Attract and Hold Men
Sexual Slavery of Women
Essentials of Happy Marriage
The Sex Organs

There is no longer any need to pay the *awful price* for one moment of bliss. Read the scientific pathological facts told so bravely by Dr. Rubin. The chapters on venereal disease are alone worth the price of this book!

You want to know, and you *should* know *everything* about sex. Sex is no longer a sin, a mystery, it is your greatest power for happiness. You owe it to yourself, to the one you love, to tear aside the curtain of hypocrisy and learn the *naked truth!*

New. BIRTH CONTROL FACTS

FREE! AMAZING NEW BOOK ON NATURAL METHOD OF BIRTH CONTROL

AWAY with artificial devices! Nature offers a dependable, healthful method of controlling conception as recently proven in startling scientific tests. The famous Ogino-Knaus theory of rhythmic birth control is explained in detail and includes a complete table of fertile periods. This book is FREE with orders for "Eugenics and Sex Harmony"

PIONEER PUBLICATIONS, INC.
Radio City, 1270 Sixth Ave., New York City